SWEET Demon LOVE Baby

Join our mailing list at

palmcirlepressbooks.com

to receive an unforgettable
FREE short story. Plus news and contests!

SWEET *Demon* LOVE *Baby*

SOUTH BEACH CRIME THRILLER

BOOK TWO

HEATHER WILDE

Printed in the United States of America

ISBN: 979-8-9888754-0-6

Book Design by Oladimeji Alaka

Front Cover Image by Subbotina

Interior Layout by Rachel Newhouse for elfinpen designs

Published by Palm Circle Press
www.palmcirclepressbooks.com

For Mark

"Death is the dropping of the flower that the fruit may swell."

— HENRY WARD BEECHER

One

Naked, Nora Montoya got onto her hands and knees. She picked up the dollar bills which had been tossed onto the stage around her. Collecting her earnings like this was a bit demeaning, but better than letting some sleaze trace your thigh with his dollar like this actually turned you on. She had her pride.

While making the one-on-one rounds afterward, she noticed her boss Jason Shaw walk in. He glanced at her, smiled, winked. Even through a hive of patrons and nude dancers, everyone swathed in black light, he could pick her out. Her heart skipped. He kept looking at her with this suspicious glare as if he knew what she was up to. Because of course he knew. How could she have hoped to date a cop without Shaw finding out?

She watched Shaw disappear around the corner of the hall. She crossed herself, then nudged her way to the dressing room. She opened the red door there and paused in front of the mirror inside. "Look at Your-self," a print-out read, taped above the frame. The mirror was meant as a last inspection point for danc-ers before hitting the stage, offering them a head-to-toe view. Nora found herself inspecting, even when her dance was over. She wasn't skinny but managed enough kickboxing and yoga to keep her Latina curves contained to her breasts and hips. She kept her olive skin at a level shade throughout her body, even her bikini area. No tan lines made for better tips for whatever stupid, psychological reason.

Nora parted the beaded curtains and entered the dressing room. Valerie sat in the closest chair, hunched over its dressing table, using her nail polish bottle to crush pills into a powder. Suzie touched noses with her reflection, applying lipstick, already high herself. Double-D Deborah came out from the bathroom, toilet draining noisily behind her.

Before Nora could organize and count her money, Lionel stabbed his immense head between the cur-tains. His hair was shaved into a cap, his lower face hidden by a fluffy neckbeard. Lionel was Shaw's head of security. "Yo, Nora! Boss wants to see you."

Here we go. Nora's knees tingled, and her spine and chest became hot. She'd had nightmares over this moment.

She stepped into a G-string, not bothering with a top. She decided to hold her money. Let Shaw see it. Remind him what a good earner she was. She left the dressing room and weaved her way towards the office. A drunk man tried snatching her for a hug. He leaned in like he wanted to tell her a secret, but she peeled his arms away and kept walking, ignored the snarky comments hurled at her back. She went through another set of beaded curtains, through the "Employees Only" door, down the next hall.

Lionel, all six feet-four inches of him, stood there waiting for her. He opened the door for her. He shut it after she walked in.

Shaw sat at his desk. His office looked more like a stock photo of an office, rather than an actual workspace. The papers on his desk were stacked in such alignment as to resemble a solid box. Shaw himself matched this motif, all smooth surfaces and sharp corners. His face was tan, but not overdoing it, like a lot of Miami men in their fifties. His beard was manicured so skin-short it appeared drawn there. A black, button-up shirt and black slacks wrapped his slim frame like a super villain uniform.

"Have a seat," he told her.

There was only a single, white, plastic chair available, so she pulled it up and sat in it.

"How have you been?" he asked her.

She smiled, coughed, laughed, caught off-guard. "Um, okay. Thanks. You?"

He lifted a clipboard from his desk and paused from the sight of it, as if it presented him with an unexpected math problem. He lay the clipboard down again. "Look, Nora, I need your help."

"Sure, anything. I'm always happy to help you."

"I have some new girls coming in Saturday night. Five of them."

He seemed to expect a response from her. She said, "Okay. Five girls. From where?"

"A couple of them are from China, I think. Not sure about the rest yet. They speak English, but it would be great for them to have an ambassador. Know what I mean?"

"You want me to chaperone."

He looked briefly at the ceiling while choosing his words. "A little more than that. I want you to teach them. Make them understand what's expected."

"Okay, but why me?"

"Dara doesn't like doing it anymore. I promised her I'd find someone else." Dara was his personal assistant who also happened to be Lionel's twin sister. For reasons no one could agree on, Dara was a maternal figure to Shaw, the only living being capable of influencing him. "Besides," Shaw said, "I want you to show them what a success story you are. Show them what they have to look forward to. Can you do that for me?"

He searched her eyes, and those ice-blue irises pierced icicles through her soul. Success story? Her? What the hell was he talking about? Evidently, for him, she was the most success any woman could ever hope for: work as a call girl for a few years, transfer to stripping when that wore out, keep your figure, or go work the register at some small business until you died. His restaurants always needed waitresses, so there was that.

"Sure," she said, "I can do that. I'll teach them."

"Fantastic. That makes me happy, Nora. You're an angel."

"Anything else?"

He smirked, shrugged. "*You* tell *me*. Anything else? Everything all right?"

"Absolutely."

"You've been quiet and standoffish with me lately."

"Have I? Sorry. Didn't mean to."

"Don't I make you feel good?"

"Of course, yeah."

"Then we have no worries. I'm having a pool party in a couple of days. Why don't you come by?"

She agreed to do so, reminding him he'd already invited her.

"Cool, cool. See you there, Nora. I'll be in touch when the girls arrive, okay? Thank you again."

She left his office and stood outside with her hand on the doorknob. She released a big breath and used a hand against the wall to help herself walk. She still held her money. He hadn't even glanced at it.

Nora was scheduled for one more dance. Afterward, she was going straight home. She would call her sexy, handsome cop boyfriend and dump him. She couldn't keep going like this, especially if Shaw was going to make her work more closely with him now. Also, he'd noted a difference in her behavior. No, her relationship with Trace had become far too dicey. She could no longer manage the pressure of a secret relationship with someone not even aware it was a secret.

Combined with Trace's tendency to sometimes overdrink, the situation had sparked plenty of fights between them, some loud and rageful enough to bring her neighbor knocking, threatening to call the police. The irony. It was time to end things with Trace the Detective. Even if it broke both of their hearts to pieces.

—

Her apartment was only a dozen blocks to the north on Third Avenue between Collins and Washington. Nora lived in a two-story, renovated, multifamily building painted white to alleviate the uninhabitable heat of mid-summer South Beach. The studio apartment she rented was pricier than most, but its proximity to the club made this palatable. Best of all, her walk to and from work allowed her to cut through Lincoln Road, a palm tree promenade lined with shops and cafés.

When Nora reached home, she unlocked the front gate. She crossed the courtyard, a tropical landscape of bright foliage and flowers, including lots of bromeliads. She went to the far stairs to the second floor, her apartment nestled in the corner. She used a separate key to unlock the outswing, wrought-iron security door. She elbowed it open as she unlocked the main door.

She went in, turned on the lights, dropped her purse atop her bed. She sat at the chair by her desk and regarded her cellphone in her hands, distrustful of it. She called Trace, convinced he wouldn't answer this late, but he did. She flinched.

"You answered," she said.

"Sorry to disappoint you."

"It's not that. Come on."

"Want me to come over?"

She took a moment. "We need to talk."

"Something wrong?"

"I have to come clean on some stuff…about me." Nora wondered at herself for saying this. Wasn't the purpose of her call to break up with him? Instead, she was confessing.

"I'm listening," he said.

She thought of where to start, but the best beginning for doing so kept changing itself. A minute went by, and she hadn't said anything.

"Nora, why don't I come over?" he asked.

"No, I have to get this out first. It's about how I became a dancer. What I was doing before dancing."

"Okay, you don't have to do this. Maybe I don't want to know."

"I'm positive you don't, but probably you should."

"Seriously. Don't tell me. I don't want to hear this."

"You have to, Trace. It's the truth."

"I'm coming over then."

"No, don't. Don't make this harder? Please?"

"I'm hanging up." He hung up.

Nora started to curse, but her air became cut off. An arm had encircled her neck and was squeezing. She arched her back and pushed with her knees. She attempted to squirm away, but the arm had a strong hold, folded directly beneath her jaw. She tried screaming when she saw her attacker's other hand holding a butcher knife. She made a choking noise.

He jabbed the knife at her, but she moved, the blade slicing the back of the chair. Strengthened from panic, she twisted her head. She got sideways enough she could chuck an elbow into her assailant's temple. He cried out and let go. She raced for the front door, but the attacker caught her by her hair. When her extensions shredded free, she continued running. She clutched the doorknob and yanked the door open, but her attacker was right there. He slammed the door closed with both hands flat. She ducked out of his arms and ran back inside the apartment, though she didn't know where she might escape to anymore. She considered the bathroom where she might lock herself inside, but her bed was in the way. She wouldn't make it. She headed for the window instead. She was on the second floor. She could jump.

Nora only made it a few steps before he grabbed her around her waist. He lifted her, and she felt the blade enter her stomach in rapid succession. She felt the blood wetting her clothing. She stood dripping until her assailant let go, and she ran for the window again. The effort of unlatching the window and forcing it open caused her legs to give out beneath her and she collapsed.

She tried to get up again, but she could only turn onto her back. She lay looking at her ceiling fan, the blades caked with dust. How could she have let them get so filthy? She'd just never had a reason to look up there before. She closed her eyes because they felt heavy. Nora Montoya took her last breath and died.

Two

Trace awoke that next morning on the beach, massively hungover. He lifted his head and blinked from the agonizing, overpowering radiance of the sun. His lips tasted salty. His head felt cracked and delicate as an egg, his thoughts runny as yolk.

His phone buzzed from his front pocket. He took the phone out and squinted to see the caller. It was Enrique, his partner.

"Trace, where are you?" he asked.

He sat up too fast and the world tilted. His vision swam. He looked around himself. "I'm, uh, I'm taking a jog on the beach."

Enrique made a deep breath. They didn't come much deeper. "I've got some bad news for you, partner," he said. "I don't know how to tell you this."

Trace brushed sand from his knees. "Just say it."

"It's Nora, man. She's been killed. Someone stabbed her."

"Wait, wait, wait, wait, wait, wait. What?"

"At her apartment. Someone broke in last night and stabbed her. A lot."

Trace needed to throw up. He clamped his hand over his mouth.

"Trace, you there?"

He wasn't. Not anymore. He got to his feet, his entire nervous system bending inside-out. He rubbed his chest while he paced. "Yeah, I-I'm here. I'm, uh, I'm trying to process this."

"Everyone's been trying to reach you."

Trace looked at his phone. 21 missed calls. He replaced the phone to his ear.

"…couldn't get a hold of you, so they called me," Enrique was saying.

Trace felt increasingly light-headed. He dropped into the sand, his legs folded beneath him.

Enrique must've heard the impact. "Hey, you all right?"

"Are they sure it's Nora? Maybe it's not her. She has other girls stay with her all the time."

"They've identified her. I'm pretty sure."

"So what happened exactly?"

"I don't know all the details yet, Trace. Someone broke into her apartment last night. That's all I know."

"Are they sure she's dead?"

"Of course. Look, I'm sorry. I can't imagine how you must feel right now."

Trace massaged his chest again, assessing the solidity of it. "I can't either," he said.

A person jogging for real went by, completely unaware of how lucky they were to not be the guy they'd just passed.

"I'm going to her apartment," Trace said. "Right now. I'm not far away."

He heard Enrique hesitate, like he was mulling over whether he thought this was a good idea. "There's something else, buddy."

"Thought you didn't know any details."

"Only this: A neighbor says she heard you both arguing the other night. Says she hears you both fighting all the time."

"All the time? More like twice!"

Mrs. Rojas, Trace thought. The Chilean woman who treated Nora like her own daughter. Mrs. Rojas had never cared for Trace. He could easily imagine her telling anyone who would listen that he was the likely culprit. She knew Trace was a detective, but it made no difference to her. He was a man.

Trace felt he should elaborate but stopped himself. Should he keep quiet now? Working homicide for so long, it was hard not to ever imagine how he'd handle the same situations his suspects found themselves in. Now here it was for him, and Trace felt clueless.

Enrique was still talking: "The old lady says she thought she heard banging noises, so she came over. The door was open, and she found Nora inside."

"And she says I did it?"

"Not exactly, but she talked a lot of shit about you. I'm just giving you a heads up."

Trace found his feet again and resumed pacing. "I can't believe this is happening. Enrique, tell me this isn't happening."

His partner cleared his throat, made a humming sound. "My man, this isn't the easiest thing for me to ask you, but…"

"No, I don't have an alibi for where I was last night! Enrique, I didn't kill my girlfriend."

"I'm aware of that, but there's going to be some questions. Also, her phone has your number as the last one called."

He slapped his forehead. This hurt tremendously, so he did it a few more times. "My God, I was supposed to go over and see her last night. But I chickened out and got drunk instead. Enrique, I could've saved her!"

"Hey, buddy, no. You don't know that."

"I was supposed to go over there, and I didn't!"

"Calm down. You're not helping yourself."

"I could tell she was going to break up with me. Something in her voice. I don't know. I couldn't face it. What a *coward* I am!"

"Trace,…stop."

"She's dead because of me!"

Enrique repeated Trace's name as Trace became lost in middle space. He tried to imagine Nora dead and the image wouldn't conjure. His Nora. The concept was too abstract. "You okay?" asked Enrique's voice inside his phone, communicating from another galaxy.

"I'm headed over there," Trace said. "To her apartment. I have to see for myself."

"Right, right. I'll meet you there."

Trace dropped his phone hand without hanging up. He looked out over the ocean. Warm-blue waves rolled over the smooth, tan sands of the shore. A gaping seagull flew over. Another jogger went chugging by. A blonde couple embraced one another and smooched. Trace's entire world had ended, and the world didn't seem too much bothered by it.

—

On a rare night off, three months ago, Trace had been too restless to take it easy at home. He went for a night ride on his roadster bicycle and ended up at Lincoln Road. This was a popular path for cyclists since there was no automotive traffic to contend with. He came across Nora walking by herself, and he felt compelled to pull over. Her beauty made him assume she was frequently harassed in this way, but he couldn't help it. He told her his name and offered to walk her home, using his concern for her safety as a thinly veiled excuse. Despite some mild reassurances that she was fine, really, she was fine, he used the opportunity to start a conversation. When it came out she was a dancer at The Club Cabana, he confessed to having once been a stripper himself in a former life. He'd transitioned from "Stripper Cop" to "Actual Cop." She found this utterly hilarious. Nora would even pause in their conversation minutes later to laugh about the "stripper cop thing" again. He mentioned how he was currently a homicide detective and none of his fellow cops knew anything about his past. This took some convincing on his part, but by the time he had her sold, they'd arrived at her building. He asked her out to dinner and the rest was history. They bonded over both being strippers.

He now arrived at her murder scene. Walking up her stairs, he spotted Mrs. Rojas' door crack open, her rodent eyes flickering within. Once spotted, she slammed her door shut. Trace had his own key, so he went to open her door, then noticed the police tape crisscrossing the doorframe. He would've been better off waiting for Enrique anyway. Wasn't wise to go touching stuff without a witness. Trace had a seat on the top step and resumed marveling at himself for not having come over last night. He could've saved her. If not to prevent her attack, then at least to get her the medical attention she needed. He'd committed the ultimate failure.

Across the lush, green courtyard, a trio of neighbors came out of their apartments, saw the police tape across Nora's door. They grouped together and whispered to each other. Trace heard the word "murder." One of the neighbors approached him. The neighbor wore a straw hat and browline sunglasses. He asked Trace if he knew what had happened. Trace confirmed a girl had been killed but didn't say anything else.

He stood when he spotted Enrique at the front gate. He descended the stairs to let his partner in and the two men hugged. The neighbor looked at them, confused. He turned and shuffled back towards his apartment.

"How are you holding up?" Enrique asked Trace.

"Still in shock. I keep checking my phone to see if she's called me."

"You sure you want to go in there? You'll spray your DNA everywhere."

"It's already sprayed there, I assure you."

Enrique looked at him as if expecting him to say more, but Trace had nothing else. He chewed at a hangnail.

The manner in which any death scene investigation was conducted was always a crucial factor in its success. Trace understood it would be wrong for him to go in. Though evidence had already been gathered in an initial search, secondary searches were entirely plausible. He could easily spoil the integrity of the crime scene, adding fibers, adding cells, adding tissue. But he simply didn't care. He had to go in. Though he wouldn't get to see her body in the context of her surroundings, he felt more capable of interpreting what he saw better than any other detective. Besides, Trace knew Nora had kept a diary. He would be shocked if they'd found it since it was incredibly well-hidden. He wasn't even sure where it was himself, but it was worth looking for. He also decided he'd best read it before anyone else. Just in case. Never knew what someone might misinterpret.

"So, you know," Enrique said, "Fulcher has given this case to Callaway and Paletti."

"I know. They left me messages."

"They're decent detectives. They'll find out who did this, Trace."

Trace shook his head. Actually, no, they probably wouldn't. Callaway and Paletti were a pair of racist, xenophobic meatheads. He'd frequently heard both of them demeaning immigrants like Nora. They would treat this case as another Hispanic whore who shouldn't have come to this country in the first place. Of course she'd gotten herself killed. It was inevitable. He imagined they would provide her murder with only the most cursory attention before pronouncing it unsolvable.

Trace arrived at Nora's door where he took out his copy of her key again. He used it to open the security door and the main door. Both opened inward, so it didn't break the police tape.

Trace peered into her apartment. He took in how incredibly motionless it appeared, save for a slowly swaying, oyster-shell wind chime. It clinked from a small breeze. He saw the light-gray, shag area rug in the living room and remembered making love to Nora on it. The surprising abrasions this had caused.

A corner of the rug was matted by something dark. Realizing it was dried blood, Trace about-faced and sprinted back down the stairs, three at a time. When he reached the courtyard, he leaned over and vomited while holding onto the railing. He didn't have much in him, so dry heaves came fast. His diaphragm ached from strain. His ribs, too. He'd seen the blood of murder victims countless times, but this was different. This was liquid spilled from the veins and arteries of someone he loved—yet the blood had looked the same as anyone else's, which only made it worse. He would have to come back and search for her diary later. After her blood was cleaned up. There was no other way.

Three

Shaw entered *Paul's Place Bar & Restaurant* off Florida State Road 913. He came accompanied by his assistants Dara and Lionel, the twins. They pulled up in his gunmetal-gray Porsche GT1 Strassenversion.

Paul's Place was a smallish, rectangular, cement building with an outdoor seating area arrayed with tiki huts, wicker chairs, and palm trees. Beyond these sat a striking, postcard view of the ocean, a former hideaway cove for pirates. The bar-restaurant faced No Name Harbor in Key Biscayne, its teal-green water littered with large, white yachts. Without having to look, Shaw knew the menu here would include seafood with Latin American Fusion. This was most evident from the mermaids and smiley sharks airbrushed onto the outer walls, a mural of happy seafaring creatures everywhere.

Shaw stepped inside and saw a pot-bellied man in a *Miami Marlins* cap. He sat astride a wooden stool, hunched over as he brush-coated the bar with varnish. The smell from this was pungent, almost stopping Shaw in his tracks. He forced closer until the man noticed him and sat up.

"How soon do you plan on opening?" Shaw asked him.

The man placed his brush down across the varnish lid. He wiped his hands with a rag and stuck his hand out. "My name is Douglass. You are?"

"Jason Shaw," he answered without shaking the hand.

Douglas dropped his hand, giving up. "I'm only a couple weeks away from a soft opening. I'm aiming to make the grand opening in August."

"Is the owner around?"

"That would be me."

"Well, Douglas, actually what you're going to do is shut down and go back to wherever the fuck you came from because I was going to buy this building. This is mine."

Douglas chuckled. "Beg your pardon there?"

"You heard what I said. This is my building. I was going to buy this."

"Seems you were a little too late, weren't you?"

"I'm a busy man, so the sale slipped my attention. It's true. But I'm here now and you're going to sell me this restaurant, or I'll crack every bone in your fatass, ugly body."

Douglas seemed to fully take in this man Jason Shaw, his opaque sunglasses, dressed in black despite the heat. An attractive young woman with a slight frame and light-colored pantsuit stood behind him. Next to her was a mountainous, bearded man wearing a dark, tight-fitting suit, also far too warm for the weather.

Douglas chuckled again. "Let me guess. You're the local business bully who assumes he can tell everyone else what to do because he has so much money. You think you're pretty intimidating, but really you're full of shit. Sound about right?"

Shaw grinned and stepped closer. "Who's Paul?"

"What?"

"It's called '*Paul's Place*,' but you said your name is Douglas."

"Paul's my father."

As both men spoke, Lionel walked casually over and grabbed Douglas from behind with his arm around his throat. Douglas contorted and kicked and came off his stool. He knocked over the varnish. Lionel tightened his grip while managing to sidestep the splash after the varnish bucket hit the floor. Douglas clawed at Lionel's arm. He tried twisting free, but Lionel had him. He held the owner up while forcing his head back, enough that Shaw could look into it.

"Will you take a check?" Shaw asked him.

Douglas gasped to speak but could only croak.

"I'm a restaurant owner myself," Shaw explained. "I own two restaurants right up this street. I'm also the chef. Or I used to be. Don't have as much time as

I used to."

Douglas kicked while pulling at the arm around his neck. He was choking.

Shaw reached inside his blazer and removed a heavy titanium set of brass knuckles. He slid his fingers through its loops and admired the way the brass knuckles glinted in the late-day sun, leaking through the window. "This isn't a nice thing to do to a person and for that I apologize," he said. "But you took my restaurant."

He slammed Douglas in the stomach, and he doubled over. Lionel straightened him back up again, right in time for Shaw to land another stomach punch, this one even harder. Douglas hyperventilated, at least finding oxygen from being moved.

"Do you have my checkbook?" Shaw asked Dara. "Write the man a check."

"How much?" Dara asked him. "He hasn't said. Why don't you let him talk?"

Shaw's phone chirped. He took it out of his blazer and handed it to Dara who accepted the phone. She said hello in a low voice while stepping outside. Apparently she welcomed the excuse to step away from such violent, male nonsense. She vanished into the sunlight.

Shaw turned back to Douglas, now wheezing from his pain. "How much did you pay for this place?" Shaw asked. "I'll write you a check. Is that understood, Douglas?"

The man's face turned red, arteries pumping blood

to his head, jugular veins draining. He was nearing unconsciousness.

"Loosen up," Shaw said to Lionel. "He can't talk."

Lionel released him and the man fell to the floor. He barely caught himself in time from faceplanting. He landed hard on his elbows. Dust spread out from the floor where he coughed.

Shaw squatted and ruffled the man's hair. "You genuinely thought you were going to open your own business in this neighborhood? Like that? Right under my nose?"

Douglas had no answer. He trembled. He blinked a lot, visibly trying to grasp how his day had gone from a simple, touch-up, varnish job to being physically assaulted and possibly murdered.

"In case you're thinking of going to the cops," Shaw added, "it won't get you anywhere, all right? I'm sure you will anyway but, see, the police in this town all know me. I'm a pillar of society. A Miami Icon. They'll tell you they're looking into it, and you know what they're really going to do? Not a damn thing, Douglas."

Douglas began to sob and such a display of helplessness angered Shaw. He slugged the brass knuckles across the man's face. His head yanked to the side, and he cried out. This annoyed Shaw more, so he punched the other cheek, which sent Douglas' head the other way. Blood dribbled in a gooey thread from his bottom lip.

"P-please, okay, stop, " he whimpered. "I'll do

what you want. Stop!"

The doorway went dark, which caused Shaw and Lionel to look. Dara stood there. She tucked a strand of hair behind her ear and cleared her throat.

"Sh-Shaw…," Dara sputtered, "I need to speak with you. Outside."

"Tell me here. Is it about the phone call? Who was it?"

She glanced back and forth between Shaw and the parking lot outside. She looked at the floor and said, "Nora's dead."

"Which Nora? *My* Nora?"

"Someone stabbed her."

Shaw ran his hand through his hair. "Who?"

Dara shrugged. "I don't know, Shaw."

He ran a hand through his hair again. He couldn't stop doing it. "Oh my God. Nora's dead?"

"That was a reporter who called. She found out Nora worked for you and wanted to ask you some questions."

"What did you tell her?"

"No comment. *Duh.*"

Douglas coughed and this triggered Shaw who pivoted, and karate kicked him in the chest. Dissatisfied with how weak his foot connected, he grabbed Douglas and tossed him onto his back. He kicked him repeatedly in the ribs. The man rolled away, but this only opened his back to more kicks. When he tried getting up, Shaw used his heel to force him back down again. Shaw straddled his chest and pounded his face with his brass knuckled-fist. Douglas tried turning his face away, but there was nothing he could do. His face became a bloodied mess. A few more swings and Shaw was snatched under his arms by Lionel who lifted him to his feet. When Shaw went to renew his assault on the restaurant owner, Lionel stood in his way.

"Come on, boss, hey. You're going to kill the guy. He's not worth it."

"You're damn right I'm going to kill him! I'm going to kill *everybody*!" Shaw's normally slicked back hair now stood clumped into hoops. His shirt collar had lost its shape, bunched atop his blazer. Dust crescents covered the knees of his pants.

"Boss, let's go," Lionel said in a low voice, almost cooing. "We've made our point here. We have to go meet your bookie anyway, remember? You've got those big bets waiting for you."

Shaw spun himself out of Lionel's grasp and walked aside. He smoothed his hair back down and regarded the twins. He glanced once more at the man on the floor. Douglas rolled from side to side, trying to find a position which didn't hurt, but without success. He moaned and bled.

"This is horrific news," Shaw said, addressing the room, his voice cracking. "Whoever killed her…"

Dara turned from the doorway and walked back towards the Porsche. Lionel followed his sister. He paused at the door to make sure Shaw was coming, which he eventually did. He sniffled and went to wipe his nose. However, he forgot he still wore the brass knuckles, so he accidentally punched himself.

Didn't hurt.

Four

The Miami Beach Police Station was a four-story, white structure with millions of windows, more closely resembling a hospital than a law enforcement headquarters. Serving as a centerpiece for the front walkway stood an anti-aircraft cannon, for reasons no one seemed able to remember or explain. Trace always figured it must've been simply aesthetic or symbolic because Miami Beach had never once been under threat of an aerial attack from anywhere.

Inside the left wing, second floor, he sat in Chief Fulcher's office. Fulcher had only recently been promoted from Captain after Chief Correa resigned. The deputy chief resigned with him, so that left the way open for Fulcher's promotion straight to chief. He'd seemed destined for it anyway. Men respected him — the way he carried himself, that baritone voice, the lanky physique. He also wore a bushy mustache reminiscent of a cowboy sheriff, perhaps more suited for a Texas municipality than the neon flamboyance of Miami Beach.

Trace sat in front of Fulcher's desk, marveled over how odd it felt being on the other end of an interrogation. He knew they would likely reframe this as though it were something else, but he was experienced enough to know better. Even as part of training, Trace had learned every technique: Build rapport, observe body language, note speech patterns, discourage denials. He felt nervous and wanted to get this over with.

Chief Fulcher walked in and shut the door slow behind him. He wore his long sleeve, dark-blue uniform, the chest area extravagantly adorned with brass badges and horizontal insignia. He also wore a dark-blue tie with gold tie-bar and leather gun-belt. Trace wore white cargo shorts and a tan T-shirt from a tourist store sales rack.

Fulcher took his chair behind his desk, every movement calculated, deliberate, as if afraid the wrong movement might trigger Trace and cause him to shoot up the office. For the first time ever, at least from what Trace had seen, Fulcher seemed uncertain of how to proceed with the task at hand.

"How you feeling, Trace?" he asked him.

He rubbed the arms of his chair. "Seems unreal."

"I'm going to put you on leave, okay? Until the investigation is over."

Trace took a moment to evaluate this information. He knew a forced leave could be a possibility, but he felt stunned anyway.

Noticing Trace's confusion, Fulcher added, "It's paid leave."

"Chief, I didn't do anything."

"Everyone knows that. This isn't punishment. Come on. It's for your own good."

"I appreciate that, sir, but I am aware her neighbor said some incriminating things about me."

"She did. She said the two of you were always fighting."

"Mrs. Rojas is overprotective and nosey."

"What did you and your girl fight about?"

"She was a stripper, and I was a cop. We didn't always see the world the same. That's all. Arguments happen. We were a normal couple."

"Normal?"

"I didn't kill my girlfriend, sir."

Fulcher cleared his throat, loosened his tie. "I'm sure you understand you'll still have to make a deposition."

"With you?"

"With Callaway and Paletti. I gave them the case."

"Is it so necessary that I go on leave? I'd feel much better if I could help."

"Help by answering their questions. We'll find out who did this, Trace. I promise you."

Trace nodded. There was absolutely no way he would stay out of this. The mere suggestion was ridiculous. What was the point of forcing him away? What better detective than the one who knew her best? What Chief expected was impossible.

"I understand, sir," he said. "I would do the exact same in your place."

"It's what your father would've done. I used to look up to him, you know." Chief Fulcher checked him over and Trace caught the woe in his eyes. He recognized the emotion, and he despised it—it was pity. Fulcher pitied him, as though he were someone pathetic, discarded.

"You loved this girl?" Fulcher asked him.

"Yes, sir. Intensely."

"I'm sorry for your loss. I mean that."

"Thank you."

"You seem to be handling it all right though. Keeping it together. That's good."

"Like I said," Trace snickered uncomfortably, "still hasn't hit me yet."

Trace suddenly thought of mentioning Nora's diary but decided he should still read it himself first.

Fulcher stood and so did Trace. Fulcher shook his hand, linked eyes. "Listen, if there's anything you need in the meantime, don't hesitate to come to me. I think of you as a friend, Trace. We're family. I'm here to help. Nobody thinks you did anything wrong, okay?"

Then why are you making me provide a statement?

Whatever.

—

Later that same afternoon, Trace met up with Enrique at 14th Street Beach, their newest surfing spot. South Beach had the potential for barreling, board-breaking peaks, but they needed northeastern swell conditions during high tide, combined with offshore winds. Otherwise, the ocean was like a pond, and they spent the day floating and waiting for fucking Godot out there.

Today was not one of those days. Conditions were perfect. Overhead barrels broke over hard-packed sandbars, nearly to the point of being hazardous. Trace had no doubt the big waves were caused by his needing to talk to someone about what had happened. For him, the surfing had only been an excuse to meet up. A therapeutic exercise. He needed a friend to chat with, so of course an approaching stormfront would kick up the curls.

There were a couple of times when Trace attempted a conversation, but he became knocked off his board by a large wave. He gave up talking. They surfed for two hours.

Trace grew tired and trudged his way onto shore. He planted his board into the sand. He sat and watched Enrique surfing. Trace remembered when Nora had once shown up to meet him on this same beach. She carried a surfboard she'd bought that morning, so proud of herself for having picked out such a pretty board. He felt bad but pointed out to her the board was too small. It was a surfboard meant for a young teenager or smaller. It would sink if either of them tried standing on it. Unconvinced, she tried it anyway, flopping and falling continuously, yet having the time of her life. Trace's throat hurt from laughing so hard.

His throat hurt now from remembering it. He became lost in thought until he nearly didn't recognize Enrique as the person walking towards him, surfboard tucked under his arm. He planted his own board in the sand next to Trace's. He plopped onto the sand beside him. Enrique joined his arms around his knees and dripped saltwater. The two homicide detectives sat in silence. They watched the rough surf toss itself around, foaming and hissing.

"How you feeling?" Enrique asked him.

"I guess there will come a point when people stop asking me that."

"Sorry, but I don't know what else to say to you, bro. I can't imagine how you feel."

"Me either. I wish someone would tell me."

"How did the interrogation go?"

"Thank you for acknowledging that's what it was."

"They were dicks?"

"They enjoyed it, yeah. I don't know why. I never did anything to those guys."

"Maybe you're taking it too personal?" Enrique wiped his face with a towel, which Trace noticed for some pointless reason was not a beach towel but an actual bath towel from home. Enrique wore shades though Trace hadn't seen him put them on. He was losing his power for detail. Could he even be a detective anymore? Maybe this tragedy would cost him his job, neutralizing his skills. He was a damaged man. He could even feel Enrique looking at him differently, same as everyone, seeking some sign. Did he do it? Could he have? Just maybe?

Trace knew—deep down—he deserved this. He had gotten a reputation, formed by a history of mishandling his drink game. Women were a weakness. Enrique owned more reason to doubt Trace than anyone since he'd witnessed the worst of him.

"You're going to be fine," Enrique said. "Why don't you help us out with the club? It'll give you something to do."

"I can't help with a nightclub right now," said Trace. "Not even a little bit. Sorry."

"Give me a good reason."

Trace dropped his head, blew a small laugh. "Because when I was a little boy, I remember the first thing my grandfather ever said to me. He put me on his knee, and he told me, 'Sonny, never do a real estate deal with a cokehead.'"

"My brother's not a cokehead. He stopped that."

The nightclub Enrique was opening with his brother Reymond was once called "Avalon." Enrique had lucked upon the chance to buy the beachfront nightclub, located at the tail-end of Ocean Drive, touching property lines with South Pointe Park. A prime spot if there ever was one. His plan was to open a new club with his brother who would relocate from Venezuela. It had always been a dream of theirs to run a bar or restaurant together, which they would combine with the nightclub. Enrique had used his life savings and good credit, along with his brother's money, to secure a business loan. This would cover the renovations, but other startup costs were lacking. This left the brothers desperate for a third investor.

Chief Fulcher was a possibility. They preferred Trace, but he was in no shape to help an old lady cross the street, never mind opening a nightclub.

Trace had been to the place on a few occasions, simply due to its proximity. The size was impressive. With the number of staff and maintenance needed for such a business, Trace worried Enrique was getting in over his head. Before he could ever confide this, however, renovations were underway. Too late.

"I doubt I'd be an asset to anyone's project right now," Trace said.

"Looks like we'll be bringing in Chief Fulcher then."

"He's definitely interested?"

"Says he is. Why not get back in good with the chief? Help us start this thing. Become his buddy."

"Kiss his ass, you mean?"

"It's what I would do."

"Aren't you nervous about bringing him in? Conflict of interest and all that?"

"You know anybody else? I'd love their phone number." Enrique sighed, instantly exasperated by this line of argument. He got to his feet and tugged a black, vintage Doors T-shirt over his head, Jim

Morrison's pouting face towering above his band-
mates.

"Sorry to split on you," Enrique said. "Got some
things to do."

"Picking up your brother at the airport?"

"No, that's tomorrow morning."

"What's the nightclub going to be called anyway?"

"Ready for this? '*Sweet Demon Love Baby*.' Sign's
getting made as we speak."

"*Sweet Demon* what?"

"My brother's idea. He loves to annoy Mom because she's so religious."

"He's that kind of guy?"

"Since birth. Chief is even coming with me to pick
up Reymond in the morning. Wants to meet him."

"You'll put in a good word for me?"

"I'll also find out what's being said and let you
know. Make sure nothing is being hidden from you."

Trace picked up a miniscule seashell and flung it.
"Fourteen years working for this department, and
this is how I get treated. Like an outcast. Like people
have to hide things from me."

Enrique walked to where his light-blue cruiser
stood chained to a metal rack. He unlocked the bike
and walked it back over.

"What are you going to do?" he asked Trace. "Stay
out here? You should go home."

"Go home and do what?"

Enrique dug his big toe into the sand. "I don't
know. Whatever you decide to do, partner, take it

easy, okay? Real easy. Call you later."

He watched Enrique push his bike across the hard sand and onto the pavement. He swung his leg over and paddled, his sandy bath towel riding his bony shoulder, one hand steering while the other held his surfboard. He struggled with the imbalance for a few yards but soon found a rhythm and eased away. He blended into the Ocean Drive traffic, the twilight sky a velvet backdrop for pastel-striped hotels and feathery palm trees tall as flagpoles. Hip hop music thumped from a gold-painted convertible, cruising paradise for more fun.

Five

Trace dreamed he sat on a wooden porch overlooking a glorious mountain range, spread before them like large molars beneath a cloudless, blue sky. He sat in a rocking chair next to Nora, both of them holding hands. Trace's father opened the front door of the cabin and came out onto the porch, dressed in his police uniform. His father was younger with no gray in his hair. He regarded their view and let out his breath. He said, "Whelp." He walked over and lifted Nora in his arms. He moved towards the front railing as if to throw her off. Nora's face showed no expression, as though she were at peace with this. Trace bolted to his feet and ran to stop his father as a deafening, repetitive noise filled his eardrums. Trace clutched his head and tripped.

The noise transformed into Trace's phone alarm. He fumbled with the phone, dropping it. He refound it on the floor. He killed the alarm and tried falling back asleep, but he could smell Nora's shampoo on the pillows. He got up and went to the couch and tried sleeping there instead. His eyes still wouldn't shut. His entire body ached from having slept on the beach, from surfing so long. Sand stuck to him as though it were part of his skin. A gritty hide. Sand even filled between his toes and coated his hair, though he'd washed both vigorously.

Trace decided the diary could wait until tomorrow. He didn't want anyone seeing Nora's lights on. Also he wasn't confident the place had been cleaned up yet. He checked the time and saw it was a little after four. Camila would be getting off soon. She was Nora's best friend, a fellow dancer at The Club Cabana. Camila lived on the bayside of the island. She would be a good person to start questioning, but he couldn't remember her apartment number, nor did he have her phone digits. He knew she got off at five in the morning, same as Nora, and it would likely take her a ten-minute taxi ride home. *If* she went straight home.

He turned on his television and watched an unsolved mystery show to waste the hour. He went into the bathroom where he finger-brushed his hair, threw on some cologne. He put on a pair of sandals and a button-down, long sleeve shirt, its white, light fabric keeping him less hot than most tank tops. After a fifteen-minute walk, he arrived at her condo building. It was a bayfront residence on Alton Road, a busy street lined with large, luxury towers. They serrated the sky, shaped like toys, plastic bricks capable of being interlocked with one another. The exterior of Camila's building was wrapped in a warm, richly veined, Mediterranean-style limestone, the broad, glass door-façade gridded with bronze.

Trace waited by the front door for twenty minutes. Right when he became convinced she'd gone to a boyfriend's or out with the girls for a nightcap, a ruby-red station wagon taxi pulled up under the *portes-cochères*. Camila got out. He'd recognize that high-bouncing, blonde ponytail anywhere. He jog-stepped until catching her at the door.

"Hey, hey, Camila," he said, careful not to make his voice too loud for fear of scaring her.

It worked. She turned her head, but relaxed, as if expecting him to be a neighbor, running to catch the door for her. When he first saw her face, he almost thought he had the wrong person though. She looked different than he'd expected. Her makeup was smeared. She'd been crying.

"Trace!" she called. She hugged him around his neck and sobbed. She held him and nearly toppled them both. He brought her back to her feet again.

She cried in his arms until Trace began looking around them. He noticed they had an audience of doormen and fellow tenants, some with small dogs, also rapt with attention.

"What's your apartment number?" Trace whispered to her. "I'll walk you to your door."

Camila straightened her legs together and lifted her

hair out of her face. She was tall and plump, curvaceous and blossoming, her lips soft and rounded as rose petals.

She spoke between blubbers: "I…I heard what happened…I didn't want to work tonight, but my bastard boss made me."

"Camila, I'd like to ask you some questions. Is that okay?"

"*Si, si,* let's go up, baby."

He walked with her through the lobby. The concierge and doorman eyed Trace skeptically since they had seen Camila crying, assuming Trace must be the cause. Camila halted at the front desk and searched her purse while sniffling over it. She gave a twenty to the concierge. She marched over and gave another to the doorman, both of whom stared Trace down as they took their tip. Frozen inside their hostile stares, Trace had to speed-walk to recapture her side. He reached her at the elevator.

"She was my best friend ever," Camila said. "Like a sister! Trace, how can this be true? *Who* did this? Do you know?"

"Not yet. Which button do I push?"

"Sixteen."

Even her elevator looked opulent. Gold, shiny walks traced a mirrored ceiling and walls. How the hell did she afford such a place? How was Nora crammed inside a rented studio by the beach while Camila owned property in a luxury, high-rise by the bay? Weird.

Camila searched her purse for a tissue. Tears dripped from her jaws and onto her collarbone.

Arriving at her door, Camila fished her keys out from the bottomless, tiny purse. She unlocked her apartment, and they went in. He felt amazed by her apartment's size, at least a thousand square feet with a sunken living room. Floor-to-ceiling windows faced Biscayne Bay and revealed a panoramic view of the iridescent Miami skyline.

Always a woman of broad, dramatic gestures, Camila slung her purse across her glass coffee table. It knocked a small stack of documents to the floor. The top two were bills marked "Unpaid" and "Final Notice." She dropped into a small, plush couch nearby and sagged from another sobbing fit.

He'd underestimated Camila's closeness with Nora. They were so different and hadn't been hanging out as much lately. Nora had mentioned how flighty and moody Camila could be. Nora loved her, of course, but much preferred Trace's company.

He had a seat on the couch with Camila. He took one of the flower-designed couch pillows and held it in his lap because it was squishy, and it was there.

Camila brought her knees together and planted her feet firm on the floor. She straightened her back, suddenly defiant. "So, what, you're here to ask me questions? To investigate? Go ahead. I don't know anything."

Rather than talk to the side of her head, Trace got up and sat in the chair across from her. "Camila, you have to help me out here. I want to catch who did this. Don't you?"

"But I don't know anything."

"Not one idea? A customer from The Cabana maybe? Some creep who paid too much attention to her?"

"No, nobody. Everyone loved Nora. *Everyone.*"

"People are crazy though. Maybe someone loved her too much?"

"There is no one. Not that she ever told me about."

"When was the last time you saw her?"

"Three nights ago. At the club."

"Did she act different?"

"Different how?"

"I don't know. Scared maybe? Nervous?"

Camila creased her eyes. She nodded slow. "Maybe. A little. But she didn't say anything to me about why and I didn't ask her. I should have. I know I should have, but I didn't." She rested her head in her hand. "My poor baby…"

Trace took her hand in both of his, bringing her attention back to him. Her wet eyes met his and he held them before looking over and noticing their reflection in her windows. The two of them sat together on this sofa, their bodies and surroundings transparent. They floated above Miami like saddened, wingless angels.

She coughed. "Trace, I have to tell you the truth about something, okay?"

"That's what I'm doing here, Camila. If there's

anything to tell me, now is the time. Don't hide anything. *Please.*"

"But you're not going to like it. I was never supposed to tell you."

"You're freaking me out. What is it?"

"Nora and I, we were part of the same…group."

"This is what Nora tried telling me that night. What happened? I can take it now. I have to."

"We were kidnapped, Trace. From our countries. When we were both thirteen. I think Nora might've been twelve."

Images flashed through his mind of Nora and Camila being dragged from their homes, forced into the back of a van, both kicking and crying. "You mean …you were both sex trafficked?"

At this phrase, Camila collapsed into renewed paroxysms of sobbing. She leaned into his arms and surrendered the full weight of her body into his. Her faint, citrus smell, the pillowy plumpness of her chest against him. He felt aroused. *I am such garbage,* he thought. *The love of my life gets murdered and here I am getting aroused by her grieving best friend.* It wasn't appropriate. Nora had repeatedly teased him with the idea of a threesome with Camila, but Trace would always brush the idea off, assuming her offer was a disguised fidelity test.

He touched Camila's forearm. "Tell me everything. Go ahead."

Camila settled her head into his shoulder. She pressed the bridge of her nose against his neck, and he could feel her breath on his skin. It felt incredibly hot, like she was boiling inside. "You meet a man, nicely dressed," she said. "All charm, always knows the perfect thing to say, treats you like a queen. You move into his house with him, and rather than sharing his bedroom, you're shoved into a room with a half-dozen other girls, and your new life is explained to you. You're working for The Boss now. He's going to take care of you and give you everything you want, but you have to do whatever he tells you. No matter what it is."

"And this happened to Nora?"

Camila nodded.

"You both were forced to have sex with other men?"

She nodded.

"Nora was…raped, then forced into prostitution?"

"I wasn't supposed to tell you about it. Ever. She was too ashamed. I'm sorry, Trace. I told you that you didn't want to hear this."

"I absolutely don't. Keep going."

She spread a hand across his chest. "We both worked into our twenties, see, then we had to step aside for the younger girls. And that was it. We were released. Some girls go back home. Most girls, like Nora and I, we couldn't. There was no going home."

"So you became strippers?"

Camila lifted her head, so their faces nearly touched. "You have to find who killed her, okay? You're right. I'll bet it was some psycho customer.

They're everywhere."

Trace took a deep breath, held it, let it out slow. "This is…wow. I feel like an idiot."

"How could you have known?"

"I'm a detective. I should've seen the signs. Recognized some…red flag. Something."

Camila moved her naked leg across his. Her smooth, brown limbs shimmered pleasingly beneath the condo's track lighting. She traced his left ear with her finger. "Are you upset that I told you? This is the only way I know to help you. For you to know this. About Nora."

"I would've found out anyway…I think."

"Nora loved you so much, Trace. She thought you'd leave her if you knew. Most guys would."

"Explains why she was pulling away from me."

Camila's hand eased beneath the waistband of his shorts, sliding lower, searching for him.

He went stiff as lumber, mortified. "Camila, what are you doing?"

"I can't take it, Trace. I can't believe she's dead. She was my sister, and I want to die, too! I think about having to go through tomorrow and the next day, and I don't want to do it. I want to kill myself."

"I think we both need to pull ourselves together."

"I think we both need each other." She tried pulling down his shorts, but he had to help her.

"Camila, I don't know…"

"Are you uncomfortable with this?" she asked him.

"It's an odd way for us to be grieving."

"Nora would want this. I have absolutely no doubt. I know her. She wouldn't want us to suffer."

"She's watching us," he offered. He meant it as a question, but sounding more like he was trying to convince himself.

For the first time that evening, Camila smiled. "Of course she is, Trace. She's with us. She's standing right here and she's watching. She's enjoying."

Camila lay back on the couch, and he pulled her panties off. She bent her legs tight against her chest.

(Letter written by Anja Stanković, translated from Serbian.)

Dearest Baba:

I know none of you approve, but I've decided to go through with it. You said it yourself once, Baba. You only get one performance on this stage. There's no encore, no do-overs. I've got a few thousand saved, and my friend Natasha is going to lend me the rest. I know you think I'm being careless, but I believe this opportunity is worth the risk. What else is there for me to do here? What other hope do we have? You and Momma aren't getting any younger. None of us are, and I can't stand watching both of you suffer anymore at that horrible factory.

Ever since Dada passed, we work so tirelessly just to keep the lights on. Me and Andres and Ivana sell what we can at Trg, but it's nothing. This is a real chance to at least do SOMETHING, so I have to take the trip. I have to.

Uncle Semmy tells me I would be stupid not to go. Tells me I won't have this tight ass forever. Sounds bad in a letter, I know, but you understand how he is. He means well and he's being realistic, more so than Momma anyway. That's all. Uncle Semmy wants the best for me.

Anyway, I promised Momma and I'll promise you, too--no nudity! I won't do anything to shame the family. All of the pictures they've taken of me so far have been VERY professional.

Besides, can you imagine me in Miami? Seems like a fantasy! How could a trip like that be bad for me? "Traveling is good for the soul." That's from you as well.

Anyway, whatever happens, I love you, Baba. I will write to you again real soon. Please, understand. And don't worry!

Your Anja

Six

The serial killer paid at the door and entered the smoky, neon netherworld of The Club Cabana Strip Club. Inside was lit in mostly black light, except for the stage where spinning disco balls, LED spotlights, and spinning head lights combined with undulating female flesh to create a sensory extravaganza overload. The place stayed busy.

He had a seat at the bar where a few nude girls sauntered by, ignoring him. It was a sad night. Too many C-section scars. Time ticked slowly towards the grave. He looked around but didn't see her. Hoped she might be in the back somewhere. He'd memorized almost all of the dancers' schedules, but hers had become sporadic lately. Problems at home maybe.

He visited the club at least twice a week, which he supposed was enough to make him a "regular." He was addicted to the old school hip-hop the DJ's played, the pretty strobe lights, the voluptuously vulnerable women with no clothes on. However, the artificiality never escaped him. He accepted they would never commit to his well-being, no matter how many times they emptied his wallet.

These women served a more important purpose for him. They were targets for his agenda. This was why he'd killed Nora, his previous favorite. Followed her home, snuck in behind her, stabbed her. Nothing to it. Here he stood, all this time later, and he felt fine. Was back in the same club even, fearless. He knew he would eventually get caught, of course, if not killed himself, but his mission was more crucial than his life.

These girls couldn't help being born who they were, but this didn't stop them and their kind from taking over his country. Went to a department store yesterday and he had to go through *three* salespeople before finding one who spoke English. How telling was that? America was becoming a one-party state, and he had to stop it. Halt the invasion. He chose strippers as his victims since they were somewhat obligated through their job to fraternize with him. They presented less of a physical challenge than a man would. He would've used prostitutes, but their escort agencies actually did a thorough job of following up where the girls were and who they were with. Too risky. Street hookers tended to be toothless crack addicts, so he wanted nothing to do with them.

He'd tried joining the organization his father

belonged to, but they rejected him for his age. He wasn't even old enough to be in a strip club, but fake IDs were easy to make. (All it took was Teslin paper, a scanner, printer, photoshop, and laminate.) He felt confident his father would be proud of him for what he was doing, though he likely would never allow himself to show it. His father's line of work exposed him constantly to the truth about immigrants more than anyone. They didn't just pose an economic threat, but they also brought higher disease rates. They eroded our nation's identity with their inferior culture, religions, and values. They were an infestation which needed exterminating and only a few special men would ever be brave enough to do something about it. To restore the nation's purity.

He saw her—Starr. Not her real name, naturally, but she was a new favorite since she looked white enough, despite being Cuban. She stood five-foot-one, alabaster skin contrasting her cherry-red lips. Her large, brown eyes sparkled. They were framed inside a cascade of tight curls, which tumbled over her shoulders, like flourishes in a racing river. She took his breath away.

Starr walked by, caught his eye, smiled at him. "Hi there, handsome," she said.

"I was hoping you would be here tonight."

"Buy me a drink?"

"I'll buy you anything you want."

"Vodka and tonic. Are you sure you're old enough?"

"I get that a lot. I'm actually thirty. If you can believe it."

"I guess."

He turned around to find the bartender and did a double-take. He froze, then relaxed when he saw the bartender's profile. He could've sworn she was the girl he'd killed the other night: Nora. They had similar hair, same body type.

Starr had seen his reaction. "You all right?"

"That bartender. She looks like Nora, doesn't she?"

"Behind a dark bar, sure. It's so horrible what happened to her. Do you have any coke?"

"Plenty, but I didn't bring it with me. Want to get out of here?"

She scrunched her face. "Not supposed to."

"I can understand. After what happened to poor Nora? You girls need to be careful."

"Shit though. I sure would love some coke. Can you wait an hour for me to get off?"

"For you?" He laughed, like the suggestion was so easy. "Anything."

—

She kept him waiting an hour and twenty minutes, but he didn't care. He would've waited all year.

He maintained his patience while she said goodnight to a hundred different people. Afterward, they stepped out of The Club Cabana and onto a mostly barren Washington Avenue, no longer the alley of nightclub life it used to be. The greed of local business owners was transforming South Beach into a gameboard of overpriced tourist traps.

He walked arm-in-arm with Starr to the parking lot directly across the street. He opened the passenger door of his black, coupe-style car for her, a high school graduation present from his parents. He jogged around and got into the driver's side, exuberant from the evening's new potential. He never imagined in a million years that any of the dancers would voluntarily leave the club with him somewhere. This was providence, true and simple. How could women be so stupid?

He started the car, gave it some gas, revving it, hoping this impressed her. Starr failed to react, however, only concerned about finding cocaine.

He backed out, pulled forward, and away they went. He drove them past downtown Miami, through Coral Gables, and continued on US1. The streetlights became less and less frequent. He could sense Starr beginning to feel something was wrong.

"Hey," she said. "Where are we going?"

"Down south a little bit. I have to buy it first."

She settled into her seat, crossed her arms. "You're not going to take me out to the Everglades and kill me like you did Nora, are you?"

He looked at her, stunned. Did she actually know or was she teasing? "What are you talking about?"

"Are you the person who killed Nora and now you're going to kill me?"

He decelerated and pulled the car over to the side of the road. They were in the middle of nowhere. Crickets chirped. The engine ticked.

Starr sighed. "Oh no."

"I have something to confess," he told her while looking straight ahead.

"I don't know your name," she muttered. "Does anybody? That's how you're going to get away with this, right?"

He looked at her. "Everything's okay. Relax. My confession is that I don't do coke, and I wouldn't know where to find any, even if I wanted some. I just wanted to go for a drive with you. I'm sorry. I'll take you back home. Where do you live?"

She hesitated, watching him. "Seventy-Seventh Street."

"Can I ask for one small favor though?"

"Um, okay."

"Can I have a hug, Starr? I could use a hug."

"Of course. Anytime. I love to give hugs."

She leaned over and she embraced him, patted his back. He hugged her back, squeezing until the moment lingered and turned awkward. She sat back in her seat and eyed him carefully. Satisfied, he started the car and waited for a pair of northbound trucks to pass. He turned his car around. Rattled from her calling him out, though she'd only been bluffing, he headed back towards South Beach. Hopefully the story she would tell anyone about this incident might exonerate him, at least for a while. If he was the killer, then why hadn't he killed Starr when he had the chance?

He would save her gruesome murder for another night. He relished the power he felt from temporarily sparing her life. Even God was merciful when He wanted to be.

Seven

Enrique sat inside his midnight-blue Mustang Boss 429, one of the rarest and most highly valued muscle cars ever made, originally designed to outrace Chrysler's 426 Hemi. Chief Fulcher sat in the passenger seat, sunglasses wrapping his face like a space-age visor. They were on their way to pick up Reymond, Enrique's brother, but were interrupted by a train crossing West Dixey Highway. After the train passed, Enrique continued towards I-95. Less than thirty minutes later, downtown Fort Lauderdale lay on their right, a bundle of mirror-windowed skyscrapers. The two lawmen soon became lodged into standstill traffic.

"Such a shame to have a machine like this on a road like this," Fulcher pointed out. "I can feel that engine."

"Tickles your balls, right?"

"You need to take me out on an open road with this

thing."

"One day soon, yeah. Sorry I never offered."

Fulcher looked at him, as if on the margin of commenting about this but turned his attention out his window. It was a hot, muggy day.

"This shouldn't take too long," Enrique assured him.

Fulcher shrugged. "I took the whole day off. Going to a friend's party after this. I would invite you both, but it's kind of an 'invitation only' deal."

"I need to check the club's renovations later anyway. Also, my brother's going to want to see the club. He never has yet."

They later exhausted all avenues of small talk. The awkward interval lasted another few minutes before Fulcher asked, "Can I let you in on a secret?"

"Is this about my partner? Is he in real trouble?"

"I'm told his interview was shaky. Trace might've been a little too honest."

"He didn't kill that girl, sir. You do realize that, right?"

"Trace isn't much of a detective. He's too haphazard and reactive."

"He's been under some stress."

"You know he used to be a stripper himself, right?"

"You're kidding me."

"Wish I was."

"Like a *Chippendales* type of thing?"

"How the hell would I know?"

"Doesn't matter. I'm telling you, sir: Trace is a solid

guy. He's always been there for me. Maybe he's not perfect, but none of us are."

"I appreciate your input. I'll take it into consideration."

Enrique thought back to his fistfight with Trace. How long ago had that been? At least a couple of years. He could still feel the throbbing of his swollen testes from where Trace kicked him. He hadn't meant to but, in the chaos of struggle, shit happened. That was a different time though. They were different men. Weak men made stupid from a beautiful woman playing them both against each other.

"He loved that girl Nora," Enrique said. "He wouldn't lay a finger on her."

Fulcher cleared his throat. "What we do is serious, and I can't have detectives making the news because they're mixed up with girls like that. I'm cutting Trace loose. I have to."

"I wish you would reconsider, sir."

The traffic began moving somewhat. A breeze blew in through their windows.

Fulcher spit on the road. "We have bigger problems than Trace. We also have Jason Shaw to worry about. He has a restaurant right down the block from your club."

"There's enough business to go around. Anyway, our place is different."

"You don't know Jason Shaw like I do. He's a menace. He's dirty."

"You're not having second thoughts about investing with us, are you, sir?"

Fulcher grinned. "Not yet. I *am* curious to meet your brother though."

"You'll never meet anyone else like him."

"By the way, I'm going to need a letter from you, officially notifying the department about your nightclub."

"In case my work slips, you'll have a more solid case for firing me."

"Something like that. It's a formality mostly."

Enrique noticed where one of the buildings in downtown Fort Lauderdale was fully mirrored, reflecting the same blue as the sky. This created the illusion that the taller, wider building behind it was hollowed out in the middle. This gave Enrique pause until he realized what he was looking at.

He gave his attention back to the interstate. "I do have to warn you about my brother, sir," he said. "He can be overbearing."

"Disclaimer noted. I can handle him."

"I'm not sure if *he* can handle *you*."

"Because I'm a police chief? You told me his record was clean."

Enrique swallowed. He focused on driving since traffic flowed normally now. Wasn't far before traffic slowed again.

"Enrique,…you told me his record was clean," the chief persisted.

"He's cleaned it up, yessir."

"What kind of record does he have?"

"A few bar fights. Nothing huge."

"And?"

"A parking ticket from a bad wreck."

"And?"

"Maybe a lot of bar fights."

"What else?"

"Some drugs."

"Selling?"

"Using, selling. All of it, yeah."

"So you lied to the liquor license agency."

"Nuh-uh, not at all. Reymond's name won't be on the liquor license."

"But he's on the deed of mortgage for the building. Same thing."

"No, sir, it's not. I promise."

"I'm not sure, Enrique. That's a huge caveat you're laying in my lap."

Enrique experienced the memory of another fight—his brother sitting astride another man's chest while beating the man's head against the ground, repeatedly until his skull cracked open. Blood and brain matter leaked across the sidewalk. "Reymond is a changed man," he said. "You'll see. You'll like him."

"Sounds like the Department of Alcohol and Beverages might not."

"I apologize for not disclosing everything before, sir. This has just always been a dream of ours and you offered to invest right when we were desperate and about to probably lose everything. That was all I focused on."

"I'm only considering this crazy idea because I'd love to retire in five to ten years. I've been considering a passive income. *'Passive'* being the operative word here."

"It will, sir. This is going to be a good thing. Reymond might not always be easy to deal with, but he's motivated. And tough."

"Well, you've managed to get renovations going already. Shows me you're proactive at least. What's the name of our nightclub again?"

"Um, that's the other thing I have to talk to you about, sir."

The traffic evened out and Enrique could see the hold-up was a fender bender between a hatchback car and cement truck, its concrete mixer still rolling. Both vehicles sat well out of the way, so there had been no other reason for traffic getting clogged, except every passing dickhead's need to gawk. Marvel at the catastrophe of other travelers colliding. Everyone simply wanted to get where they were going but were stopped by others wanting the same. *Story of my life*, Enrique thought. Not anymore though.

Eight

Trace awoke in Camila's king-size bed, sweaty from the heat of a thick, down comforter. He'd slept face-down with his head turned, so his neck now felt hardened, like the muscles there had grown in a different direction overnight. Moving slow and quiet, he slipped out of bed and got dressed, watching Camila sleep as he did so. The comforter lay crumpled at the foot of the bed while a sheet wrapped between her legs and over her left breast, toga-style.

He took the elevator to the lobby and walked home by crossing Alton Road. He strolled between a pair of strip malls and cut through Flamingo Park. Its empty playground and soccer fields glistened with morning dew. He arrived at his apartment on the southwest corner of Twelfth and Pennsylvania, only a five-minute walk from the police station. He'd moved into this apartment a mere three months ago, abandoning his old place on Michigan and Fifteenth, fleeing its bad memories. This new building was a two-story, concrete block and stucco exterior structure. Very art deco. It was an improvement.

The apartment itself was a small, second floor one bedroom with a gas stove, wall unit A/C, and a combination of original, wood flooring with upgraded tile in the living room and kitchen. His bathroom was tiny, holding a pink and black motif which he found hideous but certainly functional enough.

Trace headed for his shower, but someone knocked at the front door seconds after he'd closed it. His mind flipped through an inner Rolodex of who it could possibly be, but he came up empty.

He opened the door to see a young woman, mid-twenties, with light-toned skin, her black hair stretched back into a tight ponytail, which accentuated a full-cheeked, but smallish face. She wore a loose-fitted white shirt and dark pants. In her left hand she held a leather-bound notebook, like those seen occupying the impulse shelves of every chain bookstore in the world.

"Can I help you?" he asked her.

"I was waiting in my car outside for you to come home the entire night."

"Uh-huh, and why in the hell would you do that?"

"You're Detective Tracey Strickland."

"You've been waiting to tell me my name?"

She held her hand out. "My name is Janis."

He shook her hand, then let it drop. "What can I help you with, Janis? Sorry, but I'm pretty tired."

"I'm a journalist. For *The Miami Reporter*. Your girl-friend was murdered?"

He turned into his apartment and left the door open, as if inviting her to follow him inside. With the aid of his mirrored hallway closet, he saw her walk in and close the door behind her.

"I'm going to take a quick shower," he told her. "Help yourself to some coffee."

"I'm plenty caffeinated thanks. Mind if I sit?"

"Wherever you want."

Trace entered the bathroom and gave himself a quick shower. Afterward, he realized, in order to reach his bedroom, he'd have to cross in front of her while only wearing a towel. It was either that or put his dirty clothes back on. He decided she could suffer the sight of him in only a towel for the ten seconds it would take him to make the walk. Once there, he pulled on a black, Pink Floyd T-shirt, one in which a single bar of light refracted into a rainbow by a trans-parent triangle. He also put on a pair of white shorts and cork-bottom sandals.

He sat across from her on his futon, which faced the papasan lounge chair the journalist sat on. The over-sized cushion made sitting cumbersome for her since its design was better suited for reclining. Janis ap-peared to compensate for this by leaning forward, her elbows balanced atop her knees.

"What do you want from me, Janis?" he asked her. "You here to grill me about my dead girlfriend?"

"Did you kill Nora Montoya?"

"No, I did not."

"When's the last time you saw her alive?"

"Two nights ago."

"What did you do?"

"We argued. Something tells me you know these answers already."

"Where were you last night?"

"At a friend's place. Nora's best friend. We had sex." He wasn't sure why this had come out. Wanted to see the journalist's reaction maybe. See if she was as shocked as he should've been. She wasn't.

"That's a brazen admission," she monotoned. She opened her notebook across her lap and wrote something. She spoke while writing: "Sounds as though you've moved right on with your life. Is that correct to say?"

"Putting that in your article?"

"Depends on my editor. How did...*why?*"

"It just happened. We were grieving and it made us feel better. We didn't think Nora would've minded. That seem deranged to you?"

"A little, yeah. Believing your deceased girlfriend would be okay with you having sex with her best friend, that's a little convenient, no?"

"Go ahead and judge me. I don't give a shit anymore."

"Do you have any leads on who might've killed her?"

"It's not my case. I've been put on leave. You didn't know that?"

"Why were you put on leave?"

"Chief thinks I should take a break. Take some time to recuperate."

"Are you under any suspicion?"

"Just the token amount from being her boyfriend. We have a saying in homicide: '*Familiarity breeds attempt.*'"

"Are you sure you should be saying all of this to me?"

"Why not. Get some good clickbait out of it. *Yippee.*" He sat forward and noticed his potted ivy needed water. So did his spider plant. Hell, all his plants were wilting. "Look," he told her, "I didn't kill Nora. She was the love of my life. You have no idea how many alcoholic floozies, flake-a-zoids with daddy issues, and self-obsessed golddiggers I had to wade through to find someone as special as her."

"Will you help in the investigation?"

"I gave a deposition. Not much more I can do," he lied.

"When's her funeral?"

He pinched his nose while trying to think. "Next week? I called her mom, but she doesn't want my help. Guess she's been watching the news."

"Are you close with her family?"

This brought Trace to his feet. He aimed an open hand at the door. "Hey, all right, that's enough. Thank you for stopping by."

She narrowed her eyes, caught unprepared. "Nothing else you want to say?"

"I've said way too much, I think. You caught me in a weak moment."

Janis made a shy smile. She lifted her purse from the floor. She set the purse on her lap to dig inside and came out with a business card. She stood and handed the card to him. He took the card, looked at it, studied it, like he'd once been counseled to do when taking someone's card. Never simply put it away. Read it first. Show respect.

"I am truly sorry about what happened to your girl-friend," she offered. "I hope you catch whoever did it. Or somebody does." She held his eyes until brushing her hair out of her face. She sighed. "Thanks for the interview."

"You're welcome. Go win the fucking Pulitzer."

He opened the door for her, and she left. He touched his forehead to the door and listened to her footsteps as they went down the stairs. He heard the building door open, slam shut, her footsteps carrying down the sidewalk. The room brightened from the maturing sun. He squeezed his eyes closed, surprised by a strange sound rising out of him. He sobbed, but it came out different. It wasn't sobbing. He was laughing. This wasn't the way cops were supposed to act.

Nine

Jason Shaw's mansion sat on a palatial estate. It was a wide, waterfront property with northwestern exposure. This afforded him a front-row view for daily, dazzling Miami sunsets. Private gates opened upon a majestic, Neoclassical building towering over verdant foliage. Past the front doors stood a rotunda foyer with soaring ceilings, curved marble, and a two-sided staircase with gold leaf bannisters. The three-story structure also included a rooftop terrace, temperature-controlled wine room, and a built-in saltwater aquarium, movie theatre, and glass elevator. It was nicknamed "The Sex Palace" because of his notorious parties, mostly centered around the twin, infinity-edge swimming pools.

Shaw's favorite feature of the mansion by far was the gourmet kitchen: state-of-the-art, stainless-steel appliances, gadgets galore, and a bottomless pantry always stocked with his private ingredients. Dual, commercial-quality ovens held eight-burner stovetops, industrial-strength ventilation systems, and ceramic islands with their own prep sinks.

Today's gargantuan get-together was a monthly event held for his employees. From the chefs to the dancers, right down to the busboys, everyone was invited. Families too, though they rarely came since it was widely known these parties were not suitable for minors.

Shaw had been in the kitchen since morning, cooking a feast with three of his handpicked chefs from his top three restaurants, a high honor. He worked with them on a dish of *gruyere tuiles* with puff pastry fingers sprinkled with black olives and parmesan. The main dish would be charcoal-grilled *mahi mahi* served in lemon-garlic sauce with white asparagus cut into rings and filled with black truffles. There were also crayfish with white wine and black pepper sauce and vegetables. Dessert would be candied strawberries frozen in liquid nitrogen and topped with hot strawberry jam.

He tried greeting guests as they arrived but most attempts at salutary conversation were cut short by Shaw yelling instructions at the other chefs. This happened despite some of the guests being politicians and local celebrities. Couldn't be helped. Nothing more important than the food.

He worked over the large grill pan of crayfish when he noticed someone standing only a couple feet away, as if wanting his attention without having to say anything. Shaw decided to wait this out. He was busy. The person kept watching him work, nonplussed, occasionally raising a beer bottle to his mouth. Shaw was accustomed to people observing him cook since he truly was an artist, but something about this figure made him finally look up. When he saw who it was, Shaw acted surprised for a milli-second. He turned back to the grill, turning casual again.

"Didn't expect to see you here, Captain," he said.

"I'm the chief now," Fulcher told him. "Get it right, Shaw."

"Apologies. Welcome to my home. Again."

Shaw flipped the mound of small crustaceans over, equally browning both sides. He sporadically threw in spices when intuition told him to.

"I'm here to talk some business," Fulcher said.

Shaw chuckled while lowering the grill's heat. "I've got some business to talk about myself. You catch the piece of shit who killed my girl yet?"

"You know her name?"

Shaw straightened himself, affronted. He looked at Fulcher hard. "Yeah, Nora Montoya. I'm working with her parents to arrange the funeral."

Fulcher rubbed a finger under his nose. "You don't say."

"And it's a pain in the ass because her mom absolutely insists on a Cuban Catholic church, and they only have certain days available. Plus, there's an inquest into her death, which delays things more. It's disturbing."

"Funny but I think *'disturbing'* is throwing a party a few days after she was just found stabbed to death."

Shaw whistled under his breath. The observation wounded him. "It was too late to cancel. Everything was delivered. Most of these people didn't know her anyway."

"Still seems kind of heartless to me."

"People have different ways of grieving. Mine is to stay busy. Keep my mind busy. What are you trying to say anyway?"

A slender, boulder-breasted woman, likely one of his strippers, sauntered by. She gave Shaw a grin with a come-hither look. Both men admired the shapeliness of her rear as she walked outside, her black thong thin as floss.

Shaw used his hands to scoop two handfuls of live crayfish into a pot of boiling water.

"My detectives tell me they had a chat with you the other night," Fulcher said. His attention still clung to the dancer as she moved around outside.

"At my club the other night, yeah. They were assholes."

"So you don't know a damn thing, huh? You're just so incredibly bewildered and lost with no idea about anything. Doesn't sound like you."

"I wish I knew something, Captain. *'Chief,'* I mean. I do."

"No lovesick customers? No crazy ex-boyfriends? No stalkers?"

Shaw returned to his kitchen maneuvering. "Is this why you came to my party? Continue the interrogation? Mister Killjoy? You must be popular."

Fulcher brought his eyes back inside and held his hands up. "You gave your statement to my boys. My bad. No, it's not why I came here."

Shaw noticed Lionel overlooking the guests from the interior, second floor landing. He watched anxious as Shaw spoke with the police chief. Lionel had dressed like he was at a damn black-tie party despite the thousand-degree heat and million percent humidity. He seemed to sense Shaw's nervousness but without understanding who Fulcher was. Lionel kept his hand over his stomach, poised as if ready to draw his gun from its concealed holster.

Shaw met Lionel's eyes and raised his chin to acknowledge him. Shaw shook his head quick, a signal for him to stand down. He noticed a couple, both fashion model-types, huddled in the sunken living room. They took turns bending over the walnut-brown coffee table and snorted lines. Fulcher began turning to see what had caught Shaw's attention, but Shaw prevented this by blurting the first words into his head. "Chief! Go enjoy the party, huh? Would you like your dick sucked? Pick a girl."

"Is Starr here?"

"Somewhere, I'm sure. You want her?"

"I prefer Starr."

"That she is, that she is. In fact, she is." He called up to Lionel, relieved at having a task for him to do. "Go fetch Starr!"

Lionel nodded and walked down the stairs. He mixed within the throng of partygoers, though visible since he was a head taller. Within minutes, Lionel reappeared with a young girl who looked around twenty. She wore a string bikini, which hardly hid any part of her. Her long, brown curls gushed over her shoulders, freshly fussed with. Lionel gripped her arm tight as though she might try and run away.

"Starr, you remember Chief Fulcher here, don't you?" Shaw asked her.

She glanced at the chief but didn't say anything. She looked apprehensive.

A rotund, furry man approached. He wore Hawaiian swim trunks squished beneath his enormous belly. His arm lay looped around the shoulders of a different young girl. Shaw recognized him as District County Judge Scott T. Strong. Noticing the knowing glances between the judge and the police chief, Shaw saw they bashfully recognized each other.

He nudged Fulcher's elbow. "Take her upstairs. Pick any bedroom. We'll talk business later."

Fulcher admired Starr's figure. He belched. "No, let's discuss it right here. Real quick."

The couple in the living room had begun sucking face and were helping each other out of their clothing, their entire upper lips frosted with cocaine.

Shaw swallowed. "Let's hear it."

"One of my detectives is opening a nightclub down the street from that restaurant you own on Ocean and

First."

"Sweet Something Baby Thingy. What about it?"

"So you know already."

"Little gets by me, Chief."

"Don't mess with them. I mean it."

Dara passed by them. Unlike her brother, she had seen to fit to wear a bathing suit, but without showing much. She was modest that way. The sexy librarian.

"I'm not sure what you mean," Shaw said. He turned back to his work. The water had resumed a full boil and the crayfish floated to the surface, turning bright red. They were nearly done.

"You know exactly what I mean." Fulcher leaned closer and spoke lower. "No internet trolling. No spoiled deliveries. No spies. No bomb threats. I know who you are."

"Ugly rumors, sir. Fake news. Check my record."

Starr stood nearby, silent as a post. Her large eyes darted from one man to the other as they spoke, seemingly unsure of her place in any of this.

"I might become involved," Fulcher said. "Mess with their business and you mess with me. I'm letting you know."

"Is that in your wheelhouse though? Running a nightclub?"

"Won't be going anywhere near it. It's an investment."

"So it's you and Enrique Alvarez and who else?"

"Enrique's brother...I think. We went to get him at

the airport yesterday and he didn't show up. "

Shaw snorted. "Sounds like you're off to a terrific start."

Fulcher looked down, obviously embarrassed and confused by his admission. The male counterpart of the living room couple had the girl's top off.

"Well, well," Fulcher said. He gave Shaw's shoulder a forceful nudge. "I'll let you finish cooking." He took Starr by her hand. "Remember me, sweetie?" Before she could answer, he led her towards the stairs.

Shaw caught the attention of the head of the catering staff. He made a downward circling motion with his finger, indicating the dishes on the counter were ready to be taken outside and served. The co-chefs carried the food towards the pools, which caused a delighted uproar from the guests.

Shaw was on his way to join them when a short, bulky man blocked his path, his bald head crowned by a shock of salt and pepper hair. He wore a lasso of gold chains, which snaked through his mossy chest hair.

"I need to have a talk with you," the man told him.

"Not now, Charles. It's a party." He walked by him and into the backyard.

Charles caught up. He walked backwards in front of him as he spoke, "The situation is getting serious. You can't keep avoiding me forever."

"Why not?"

"My people want their money, and I truly don't

understand why you won't just pay them. Don't you have it?"

"Excuse me. You're in the way." Shaw shouldered past him and went outside. After only a few steps, he noticed a commotion by the eastern pool. He'd assumed the cheering had been over the food, but not this time. The guests were excited by two women holding a blowjob contest. The judges were a pair of naked beefcakes who stood with their hips thrust forward, hands folded behind their necks. Most guests cheered the event while others staggered away in disbelief.

Shaw approached the contest, and a hush came over the guests, no one quite sure how he might react. He spread his feet apart and undid his zipper. He released himself while pushing his hips forward.

"The Head Judge has arrived!" He pumped his fist at the sky.

Ten

Trace walked to Nora's apartment, a trip he'd made on hundreds of occasions, though it felt understandably different this time. He took the stairs to her front door and discovered the police tape still crisscrossing it. He used his key to open the door, unsure why he'd opened the door first. Perhaps he wanted to make sure his key still worked, like it might not anymore since Nora no longer lived there.

He worked at removing the police tape without damaging it. He imagined he could replace it later. However, the police tape was too tightly wrapped and there was too much of it. He ripped it away and walked in. To hell with it.

He'd come here to search for Nora's diary, plus any other clues he might come across. The place had been cleaned, thank God. Being on leave, his access to forensics was limited. His only card was the probable existence of this diary. He didn't know exactly where her diary was and wasn't positive it even existed. According to her, she kept one wrapped in a misleading book jacket with a fake title. She'd confessed having this diary one night while they were on the subject of secrets. They'd made a pact to confess one private thing to each other.

His confession was the whole terrible story about Cassie, his ex-fiancé. After getting cold feet, Trace had suggested a small break in their marriage engagement. He'd become hesitative. Marriage meant forever, and he'd never bothered to ponder what exactly forever meant. He broke the news to her gently at a restaurant and she fled the restaurant before promptly crashing her car. The accident left her with facial scars which ended her modeling career. She filed a lawsuit against the other drivers and the city of Miami but moved to London for life as a homeless addict before a hearing could even be set. He'd ruined her life.

Nora's secret was her diary.

After walking inside, he felt the instant need to sit. He chose the sofa and recalled the last time he'd sat there with Nora next to him. They watched some movie about the "perfect murder" of all things. Trace closed his eyes and tried mentally reaching out to any lingering remnants of her aura left in this space. There was a ringing silence save for a light wind, then a dog barking somewhere far off. A car rushed by. He heard wind chimes. From a neighboring apartment, an old woman laughed, a witch-like cackle.

Trace pondered death, the true metaphysical, bio-logical inactivity of it. The abyss. With his job, of course, death surrounded him. This should've helped him understand how death related to life and what any of it meant, but it only confused him more. He believed Nora would ascend to some higher state because it was only reasonable to assume so. There couldn't be nothing; yet part of his job involved crime scenes in which the mauled corpses of much-loved, warm-hearted people lay tortured and murdered for little to no reason. This happened throughout the world every day, and often no one would ever be punished. What was the purpose of having lived in the first place? It was a frightening thought. Existence was cold and uncomfortable.

He rose quick from the sofa. He went to the kitchen, a small, modern galley with yellow-tiled floor and a drop-in sink. There were also flat-panel cabinets, laminate countertops, and white appliances. It was a visual inventory he'd never made previously, but he drank the details now, scanning every inch, trying to notice anything unusual. Nothing popped out. He lifted a drinking glass from the sink, which still had her lipstick on it. He thought about smashing it against the wall but set it back down instead.

He went to her bookshelf, which was enormous, made of dark-brown, solid hardwood. It arced over the head of her bed, twelve-foot-high at least. He stood on the mattress without taking his sandals off and, one-by-one, he removed her books from the shelves. He let them fall where they may. He paid more mind to the hardbacks since they were more likely to hide her diary.

Much of her collection would've been considered fairly heady stuff for a stripper. He read off random titles to himself: *The Stand* by Stephen King, *Jesus' Son* by Denis Johnson, *Tropic of Cancer* by Henry James. *Ulysses* by James Joyce, *Sometimes A Great Notion* by Ken Kesey, *Where I'm Calling From* by Raymond Carver. To him, her reading tastes ran wildly indiscriminate, as if she merely devoured whatever literature was at hand.

He tossed aside a row of *Vogue* and *Cosmo* magazines. He took down the last row of books and let them crash to the floor or onto the bed. As he reached the last few books, he continued believing her diary was here among them. Must have been the last book on the shelf then.

But it wasn't. It simply wasn't there. He kneeled among the pile of books on the bed and surveyed the disarray surrounding him, puzzled. He looked around the apartment and tried spying for other books. Indeed there was a large book on the seat of the furthest chair, tucked under her small lunch table. He knee-walked off the bed, knocking more books to the floor. He went to the table, pulled the chair back, picked up the book. *Linear Systems and Signals for Mass Transit Mechanical Engineering* was printed across a close-up photograph of a generic gear panel. He opened the book. The first few pages held a series of graphs interspersed with numerically-rich text. He flipped to the middle of the book and there it was—a hollowed out space containing a spiral notebook filled with Nora's scribble. Trace thought on how it was possible for this to even still be here. The only conclusion was that Callaway and Paletti were a pair of careless buffoons. So what if the title was boring? Would've taken two seconds to open it.

Trace thumbed to a random page:

Cindy thinks she might be pregnant. She's had 3 abortions with this dude. I asked her

Trace cringed. He realized how likely he was to learn more about Nora than he was strong enough to know anymore. Her inner thoughts, her truths, her warts—it was all right here in his hands.

Resisting the notion to fling the diary away, he skipped a few pages ahead. Most of the writing was in Spanish, but later entries were English. He stopped flipping when he saw his name:

Trace reminds me so much of Poppy. He's intelligent, thoughtful, handsome. Always somewhere else though. Like where he isn't is always more important than where he is. I love him to death, but he can be challenging. But the best are worth fighting for, right? He's a good guy deep down. He drinks too much sometimes, but at least he's a happy drunk. And he loves me. He cares about me. I wish there was a way for us to disappear together. Go live on a deserted island. Flee to Europe maybe. Knowing the utterly impossibility of any of that tortures me endlessly. I don't know how much more I can take sometimes. Trace, why did you have to become a police detective? There's nothing about it which suits you, except your instinct for drama. Thing is, knowing how jealous S would be makes me even hotter for Trace. No STRONGER, more passionate love than love off-limits. I can't help myself. But while a large part of me adores how much danger we're in, it's not fair to Trace. He deserves better than me. I don't want him suffering over my sins.

When should I do it though? Maybe any second. Maybe never.

Trace shut the book and let his arm drop. Yeah, this was hard. Maybe any second? *Maybe never?*

He forced himself to reopen, finger-walking back to the diary. He checked the back pages for more recent entries. He stopped when he saw an "S" again:

I saw S slap a girl tonight. Right across her face like she was a dog. If he ever hit me like that, I'd kill him. Wait, he did hit me once. Long time ago. So long that I forgot. He wouldn't do it again though. Not since I started sleeping with him. S can be the most tender man when he wants to be, but then the slightest thing disappoints him, and he goes berserk. Everyone's so terrified of him.

Sleeping with him? For how long? He checked the front of the notebook and saw it held the current year in blue pen. She'd been sleeping with someone else while sleeping with him? How had she hidden it? It wasn't possible.

He flipped to the last page while his heart hammered, and his scalp grew hot. He found it. The place he'd been so frightened to find:

I have to break up with him. The more I think about it, the more convinced I am that S would go crazy. He's so jealous of me, more than any of them. I can't be with Trace anymore and still give S the time he demands from me. As long as he wants me, I have no choice but to give myself to him. He owns me, like he owns all of us. Also, I worry he might kill us both. Wouldn't care if Trace was a cop. S has so many important people in his pockets he could probably get away with anything in this city. When I found out S had murdered people, I wasn't even surprised. He's a malignant narcissist if I've ever met one. An especially dangerous one.

Having that Dara bitch always in his ear doesn't help either. She's going to be the death of him. Of all of us. Of everything. I hate her. All the girls do. Marks my words: she's the real devil in this Hell.

God, life sucks. Why can't I just have a normal life?

The end. That was it. She'd been seeing someone else. Someone named "S" who had found out about their relationship and killed her. This diary was all the evidence Trace needed.

He experienced another gut-punch of heavy guilt.

He was supposed to come over that night but hadn't. Instead, he'd inadvertently, indirectly aided in her murder. He contemplated his next step. Contact Callaway and Paletti and hand the diary over, thus clearing his name? Or better yet, Trace could find out who "S" was and blow his brains out. He closed the diary, then closed the fake book over it. He jostled them in his hand, trying to decide.

He took his phone out of his pocket to call either Callaway or Paletti, whichever name he found first. He was surprised to discover he didn't have either of their numbers. The last thing on Earth he felt like doing was googling around for contacts, but what choice did he have? He didn't have a right to keep evidence. This wasn't his case. This wasn't his apartment. It was a crime scene he had no business in. He could likely be in trouble, no matter how valuable the diary turned out to be.

Or maybe not. Knowing these guys, they'd wipe their ass with it. Trace decided he would first visit Camila again. Find out who "S" was. Find out how this man "owned her like he owned all of us?" Who had so much power? It was preposterous.

Trace paused at the door to give one last gaze upon the home he'd shared with a human being he'd loved. Again he heard wind chimes chinking and spotted them hanging in the far window. The chimes were delicate, pink shells connected by fishing line, swaying slow in the baking, mid-day breeze. Notes lingered like bells from tiny angels.

Shaw, he thought. "S" stood for Shaw. He was the owner of The Club Cabana where Nora once worked. Jason Shaw, a well-known, high society piece of shit. Trace had never met the man but apparently the time had arrived.

Eleven

As soon as he'd pushed his way through the heavy, red doors of The Club Cabana Strip Club, Trace felt overcome with flashbacks to his own stripping days. The pumping music, the flashing lights, those dark corners, dollar bills flowering from G-string straps. He always noticed a difference though. The women he'd stripped for were typically rejoiceful, shrieking with laughter. The men inside this place sat silent and focused, like lions watching gazelles graze on the prairie. He'd always loathed seeing Nora's customers, having to face who they were and what she did for them.

A bottom-heavy hostess came up to Trace. She wore a black corset nearly shoving her breasts beneath her chin. "Don't be shy, handsome. Come on in. Nobody's going to bite you."

"I'm here to see Jason Shaw. Could you go get him?"

"You a friend?"

He flashed her his badge. "Right this second, please?"

She frowned and gave him a worried once over. She walked away and vanished beyond a beaded curtain. A few minutes later, she returned. "He's not here. He's in and out all the time. He usually comes in around midnight, if he comes in at all." She nudged her chin at the bar. "You're welcome to wait for him, but he might not even show up."

"Do you have his cellphone number?"

She swallowed hard. "I'm not allowed to give that out, sir. Not to nobody. I'm sorry."

"I'm going to find it out anyway, so it would save me some time if you told me. This is police business."

She hugged her elbows and wouldn't look at him.

"I won't tell anyone who I got the number from," he assured her. "Pretty please?"

The hostess looked at him and grimaced, still hesitating. She relented and gave him the number from memory, which surprised him. Made him suspicious the number might be fake or at least wrong. He called it as soon as he stepped outside.

"This is Shaw," a deep male voice answered.

Trace didn't know where to begin. He asked Shaw where he was.

"I'm not available," Shaw continued. His voice was a recording. Voicemail. "Leave me your number and

I'll get back to you at my earliest convenience. Thank you for calling."

He hung up and called Camila. She answered and let him know she wasn't home yet, but she would be there soon. She agreed to meet him there.

Halfway to Alton Road, he regretted not taking a taxi. It was a hot night, and he'd sweated through his T-shirt. The crotch of his underwear wasn't too dry either. As he made his way through Flamingo Park, he became bitten on his exposed skin by invisible bugs. Or it felt that way. Red spots sprouted on his skin when he scratched it.

Camila greeted him at her front door and embraced him. He slipped out of her arms and told her he needed a shower. Bad. She said she needed one, too. She took his hand and led him towards her bathroom. She explained to him how they would take this moment to work towards cleansing one another. Take a shower.

—

Enrique entered The Club Cabana Strip Club. He'd missed Trace by only an hour. Enrique dropped in twice per week, usually after any and every conversation with his ex-wife. Their union had been childless, but their split contentious. She hated his guts for cheating on her. He knew he deserved her wrath but hoped she might come to forgive him one day. Take him back even. He missed being married, the cozy reassurance of it. Enrique was lonely.

All cops enjoyed perks at strip clubs and did so mostly at *The Diamond Dixie* in North Miami Beach. Special treatment there ranged from blowjobs in private booths to sticking a finger inside here and there, long as you weren't rough. Enrique preferred The Club Cabana though because it was so much closer to where he lived. He'd known Nora, of course, but kept his distance. For him, his visits to The Club Cabana were a secret, not that he felt ashamed. Otherwise, someone might want to come with him, and, for Enrique, this was a private event. Besides, his brother hadn't shown up at the airport, so he had little else to do. (He wasn't too worried. Reymond would pop up somewhere. He always did.)

Enrique sat at the bar and ordered a cranberry and vodka. Within a minute, there was a beautiful, mostly nude girl standing next to him.

"Hi there," she said. "I've seen you here before."

"That's a bad sign."

"Buy me a drink?"

"Can I get an extra-long lap dance?"

"I don't know. Can you?"

The answer was yes.

—

Shaw drove his black BMW Alpina B10 Biturbo to *The Sands Nursing Home* on Collins Avenue. Once parked, he grabbed the flower bouquet off the passenger seat and went inside. He passed through two sets of automatic doors whisking open for him. As he entered the lobby, his phone buzzed inside his blazer for the twentieth time in as many minutes. He answered at long last, welcoming the excuse to procrastinate.

It was Charles calling each time. He sounded close to tears. "Where have you been? What is going on?"

"I'm busy, Charles. Forgive me if I'm not accessible to you every waking second."

"You need to pay these people, Shaw. They're sweating me hard, and I don't know what to tell them anymore."

"Tell them they'll get their money on Monday, okay? I've got some special imports coming in. Everything will be fine." Shaw caught the eye of the desk nurse, a middle-aged woman with tortoise shell-glasses to match her turquoise scrubs. He winked at her, and she looked away.

"Monday? I don't know," Charles was saying. "You're hurting my relationship with these people!"

"Because you keep bringing them clients? Making them money? Your people need to chill."

Charles began to protest, but Shaw hung up on him. Bookies were the human equivalent of mosquitoes, except you couldn't kill them. There were too many of them. Shaw couldn't cope anymore. Not here. Time to see Mom and get it over with.

He hit the hallway to his right. He negotiated an obstacle course of old, discarded people in wheelchairs. He visited here at least once a week, so he'd become familiar with other patients. There was the old man who never stopped clearing his throat. There was the overweight woman who ceaselessly wheeled herself up and down the hallway while bellowing for Jesus to please take her home. The sweet-faced woman who merely sat there and smiled but looking at nothing, aware of no one. He hated this place. He would've put his mother in a better nursing home, but it didn't exist. *The Sands* was rated the best in all of South Florida. Nursing homes were sad, awful places, and no amount of money could change that.

He entered Room 213. The lights were off, so he turned them on. He nearly cried out when he saw his mother slumped sideways on the bed. She lay on the verge of falling out. He tossed the flowers at the nightstand and embraced her. He lifted her up until her head settled into the center of her pillow. He fluffed and conformed the pillow until it better cushioned her. His mother opened her eyes.

"Is it time for my bath?" she asked him.

"Mom, it's me."

His mother blinked, her mouth dropping open as she tried to place him. "Jason," she said.

"Very good. That's right."

"Are you here to take me home?"

He touched her hand. He observed the thick, green vein which trailed up to her elbow. "I brought you flowers," he said.

His mother rolled her eyes and ripped her hand away. "I'm allergic to flowers, you dumb shit. Who told you to come here?"

"Mom, don't flip out."

"If you're not here to take me home, then I'm not interested in having anything to do with you. Get out and leave me alone. Useless prick!"

"You need more help than I know how to give you, Mom. Come on."

"I want to speak with your wife."

"I don't have a wife."

"What did you do to her? Murderer!"

Shaw shifted his feet and sighed heavily, dejected and uncomfortable. He massaged the back of his neck and wondered how to best handle this. Her dementia was growing worse, twice as bad every week. Bad enough that none of the nurses came running when she'd yelled about a murderer.

"I don't have a wife, Mom," he mumbled, choking some. "And you're not allergic to flowers."

—

Chief Fulcher of the Miami Beach Police Department lived in a three-bedroom, two-bath house located seven blocks from Hollywood Beach. When he arrived home that night, he entered a "shoe off" foyer, then a massive living area with large windows and a garden view.

Fulcher was greeted by Buddy, their beagle who jumped onto his legs, moving his head around as Fulcher petted him. The chief slipped off his boots as per house rules. He squatted to better stroke Buddy's head.

His son Todd walked up. He stopped short when he saw his father.

"Headed out?" Fulcher asked him.

"Hi, Dad. I guess, yeah."

Fulcher noticed an odd bulge over his son's left eye, which he first mistook for a play of shadow. A change of light revealed his son had a black eye.

He asked his son, "Did you win?"

Todd flinched at his father's touch but seemed to realize fleeing inspection would be futile. He stood patiently while Fulcher touched his son's chin. He guided his head around as he tried to get the best view. In this moment, Fulcher noticed how much his son resembled his grandfather. The father who was never available, even on weekends. The man who never shared anything about himself with anyone. Couldn't even share what it meant to be a man. Fulcher had been forced to figure it all out for himself and was never sure he'd gotten it exactly right. Becoming chief of police was the best way he knew for how to conceal this.

Fulcher wouldn't make the same mistakes with Wally and Todd. He made a point of showing respect to their mother, or any other woman in their life. He did his best to pass on solid morals and ethics to his sons. Work hard. Be nice. Fear no man.

"What happened?" he asked Todd.

"It was a girl," he said.

"It was that black girl. I told you she would kick your ass."

"No, this was Carrie."

"That tiny *spic* did that?"

"Dad, please, wow. Don't call her that."

"You shouldn't let other people knock you around. That's all I'm saying."

Todd held his hands out. "Well, I couldn't hit her back, could I?"

Fulcher nodded. He placed a hand on his son's shoulder. "You're right about that, son," he told him. "No, you certainly couldn't."

"I didn't lay a finger on her."

"That's good to hear." Fulcher patted his shoulder. Because it was. It was good to hear.

—

Camila sat on her sofa with a glass of obscure white wine, left over from some party or another. She watched her reflection floating above the undulating darkness of Biscayne Bay. She blanched at the ugly mask her face made when darkened in a reflection. She decided to flip through the photos in her phone, pausing when she came across pictures of Nora or pictures with Nora in them. This did not make her feel much better, so she contemplated killing herself. Death obviously wanted her. Surrender already. Parents were dead. Brother was dead. Most friends were dead. Best friend was dead. Why was she still here?

Trace was nice but he'd leave her soon enough. The men always left, never able to fully forgive her for getting herself enslaved in that way, to have this filthy mark on her.

Voy a ahorrar mi dinero, tal vez me mude a un apartamento más pequeño. Podría mudarme a una pequeña ciudad en el Medio Oeste, cambiar mi nombre, cambiar todo para que Shaw nunca pudiera encontrarme. Sería difícil y requeriría un montón de planificación cuidadosa, pero también puedo hacer cualquier cosa que me proponga. Tengo que hacer esto, de lo contrario terminaré exactamente como Nora.

—

The Miami Reporter writer Janis Brown sat cross-legged on her intricately-designed Gaiam yoga mat in her living room. She enjoyed some post-yoga pulls on a cherry-tinted waterpipe. She lit the mesh bowl while pushing her lips inside plastic tubing. She inhaled marijuana smoke until her lungs could no longer expand. She leaned her head back and released a fountain of white smoke, which jet-streamed against the ceiling.

She wondered if her crush was ever going to call. *A crush?* Were you allowed to call them that after college? He'd said he would call her…three hours ago. Janis pushed her left shoulder forward while stretching her head back, taking the millionth peek at her new tattoo. She'd gotten the tattoo because of him and only him. Because he'd said it would look cool. A pair of teary eyes gazing heavenward, framed by angel wings. It *did* look cool.

Still, hard to accept she'd gotten inked for life just because of his flippant opinion. Now the jerk wasn't calling her. Mother had warned her about musicians, but Janis couldn't help herself. Music was the cinema of the soul.

—

The serial killer became enraged. He spotted Starr holding hands with a Hispanic man. He wore a dark jacket with blue jeans and…was that a belt buckle? An oval, longhorn belt buckle! When the man brought her to the bar, the serial killer overheard him reminding her of his name: "Enrique" because of course his name was Enrique. Enriques were every-where, taking their part in the invasion, too. It was maddening.

Enrique ducked into a booth with her, and the serial killer considered barging in and murdering them. He would fling their sloshy entrails about the club and wake everyone up to the taker of souls he really was.

Instead he sat sulking at the bar and watched them hang out the entire evening together, neither of them noticing him, not for one second. An hour from clos-ing time, the man left. The serial killer followed him outside and across the street to the parking lot. Turned out they were parked only two spots down from each other. Life was funny.

He kept a casual distance until Enrique reached his car. The serial killer closed the distance fast, his hand inside his jacket. He gripped the knife handle, not showing the blade until he pounced.

(Letter written by Anja Stanković, translated from Serbian.)

I'm at Port Genoa in Milan, Baba. I paid and had to go straight to the airport. They wouldn't even let me go home first. It was either that or wait till next month. We took a plane and now we're on a ship. I'm with five other girls, all of them soooo beautiful, which is a relief. Feels legitimate now. Like this is a real modeling job. I'll stay in close touch though, so you can always know how and where I am. As I promised. Please, don't worry. Momma either. I know I keep writing that, but I can take care of myself. I want you to know. Besides, everything's going perfect so far.

Next time I write to you I will be in Miami. I'll be in my new apartment and we can Facetime, Baba. I miss all of you so much.

Your Anja

Twelve

Trace awoke the next morning, once again leaving while Camila slept. He made it through Flamingo Park, past his apartment, and around the corner from the police station. When he saw the horde of press outside, he ducked back. He peeked to see four television cameras on their tripods. Umbrella lights glared onto reporters in thick makeup as their sincere faces spoke some woeful news or another. Trace spotted Fulcher smoking by a side door. The two men met gazes and Fulcher motioned him over. He stubbed his cigarette into the ground with his boot.

As he got closer, Trace asked, "What's going on?"

"Someone killed Enrique."

This stopped Trace in his tracks. "On purpose?"

Fulcher closed their distance. He wiped his eyes. "I'm sorry this happened under my watch. I don't know what to say. This is the worst thing that's ever happened."

Trace took in their surroundings. The grass. The sky. The clouds. It was mid-July, a week after Independence Day, so the day would turn sizzling once the sun got higher. But for the moment it was mild, not even humid yet. Sprinklers hissed and cars drove by, and planes flew overhead. Children were starving in Africa.

"Oh my God," was all Trace could think to say. "The hell is going on?"

"Happened in the parking lot across from The Club Cabana."

"Right across the street? Is there a tie-in with Nora's murder?"

"Could be."

"Do we have any surveillance?"

"One camera, but it's shitty. You see both men from behind, and that's it. Can't even make out the auto tags."

"So Enrique's dead? Like that?"

Fulcher took a wide look around them. He made a long step forward and leaned around the edge of the building. He returned to Trace.

"I have ten minutes until the press conference," he said. He took Trace by the shoulder and led him down the sidewalk a ways. Trace resisted the urge to shrug himself free. "You promise me there's nothing you're not telling me?" Fulcher hissed. "Did you get into something bad with his brother?"

"Chief, I don't know who's doing this."

A long-limbed girl on rollerblades rolled past them.

She nearly ran into them but shouldered her way past without apologizing. From a nearby palm tree, a parrot screeched.

Trace wrestled with his train of thought. The world was insane. "I need to sit down," he said. He folded down into a patch of grass by the sidewalk. The morning dew wet the ass of his shorts and he didn't care. He fought to get his breathing under control.

Fulcher stared at him, his eyebrows knitted together. "What can you tell me about Enrique's brother? We went to get him the other day at the airport, and he never got off the plane. We have no idea where he is."

"I met him once many years ago, Chief. I know nothing about Enrique's brother except his name is Reymond and he lives in Venezuela. Has tech unlocked Enrique's phone yet?"

"No," Fulcher muttered. He looked down and Trace could tell he had no idea whether this had been done yet or not. "Working on it."

"I need to help," Trace said. "You can't expect me to sit this out anymore, sir."

Fulcher looked at him sideways. "Did you give an interview to some reporter and tell her you were sleeping with other women already?"

"Why would you ask?"

"Because she published a detailed story about it in *The Miami Reporter*. Is everything she's saying true?"

"I'll have to read the article."

"She wrote that you sat in front of her naked."

"That's a lie! I crossed the hall in front of her for two seconds. I had a towel on!"

"And you told her you understood why people might suspect you? Have you lost your mind?"

"She showed up at my door at the ass crack of dawn, sir. I wasn't thinking clear."

"Her article makes you sound like a psychopath!"

Trace squinted up at the chief, silhouetted to him by the morning sun. He shielded his eyes. "Sounds like you don't believe that assessment to be a stretch, sir?"

Fulcher scrunched his mouth. He slid the tops of his hands inside his pockets. "Trace, your record with this department has been thorny at best."

"I think my record speaks for itself." Trace climbed to his feet. "Think all of this is my fault somehow? Like, I'm wanting this shit?"

Fulcher frowned and crossed his arms. It was a small gesture, but the avalanche of condescension wrapped inside of it sparked a fire inside Trace. Brutal reality boiled over, and he wanted to explode. So fed up with misery. With being judged and looked down on. The rage became lava.

Without any provocation whatsoever, Fulcher slapped him, hard enough to spin Trace. He stumbled back and touched his fingertips to his cheek, beyond stunned.

"That was for your own good," Fulcher told him. "I know this isn't easy, but—"

"How long have you been waiting to do that?"

Fulcher put his finger into Trace's chest and pushed him. "Ever since your daddy got you this job? A fucking male *stripper*?"

Trace's fist flew from his side and struck Fulcher across his face. His knuckles grazed his cheek, but with enough force to freeze him. This only lasted a moment, however, and he tackled Trace back to the ground. The two men grappled, each occasionally landing a shot to the other's ribs. Eventually, their struggle stalemated with Fulcher atop Trace's curled body. Trace couldn't move unless he struggled harder, and he didn't want to anymore.

Fulcher went to his feet. "Get up," he barked at Trace.

Trace obeyed while brushing grass from his clothes. Tiny blades dangled from his hair. Both men wore several streaks of mud. He noticed Fulcher's left eye turning red, swelling, likely from Trace's first blow.

"Sorry," he said. He feebly attempted to help brush off his boss.

"You're fired," Fulcher said. "Dumb ass. Fuck you."

"I don't know what came over me, sir. Everyone I know and care about is getting killed."

He observed that he'd actually given Chief Fulcher a black eye, the tissue turning darker as blood and other fluids collected behind it.

"Come by tomorrow to turn in your badge." Fulcher turned away and headed towards the side door of the Miami Beach Police Department. He limped and rubbed his sides. Groaning, he opened the door and went within on his way to give a press conference covered in mud and sporting a black eye.

Trace took out his phone and called Enrique. The line rang, but no one answered.

Thirteen

Reymond Alvarez left his terminal and followed the signs for "Ground Transportation" until locating the car rental desk. He waited in line half an hour before renting a white convertible from a teenager visibly alarmed by Reymond's facial tattoos. They masked the entire left side of his face.

He used the rental car's built-in GPS for navigating him to his deceased brother's apartment. Meanwhile, he ignored the guilt chewing at him for having missed his flight yesterday. He chose to be angry. Enrique just *had* to become a cop. Had to try and save the world, didn't he? And what happened instead? He'd created a widow and a mother comatose with grief. Worst of all, he'd left Reymond alone to deal with the nightclub. And now the dream was likely over. Reymond would have to wing it from here on out. He'd improvised his entire life anyway, following what felt good and made money, so why not.

Plans never worked out.

For instance, making his flight yesterday. He'd gotten arrested for his part in a securities and wire fraud. He'd borrowed a million from a Caracas hedge fund to help start *Sweet Demon Love Baby*. In a scheme to make more money, feeling deceptively lucky, Reymond had gambled the million away, which proved not only devastating to him financially, but was illegal. After he posted bail, he used former neighborhood connections to pay off a couple of customs officers, allowing him to flee Venezuela.

Reymond's only reason for still flying to Miami was to help arrange his brother's funeral, square away his affairs, hopefully salvage the nightclub somehow. Maybe avoid jail if he could.

He took Interstate 95 South and wondered if his brother's death could be tied into the nightclub. An aggressive competitor maybe? Some crook Enrique had harassed once too often? In any case, Reymond swore to himself he would get to the bottom of this. More people would die before this whole thing was over. This much was guaranteed.

Having lived in Miami until the age of ten, he knew the fastest route to South Beach was I-95. He preferred the scenic route, so he connected to A1A at Dania Beach. He drove with the top down as warm, salty wind sang through his nose rings and flattened his blue mohawk. The bright sunshine stung his exposed temples as he cruised the beaches of Hollywood, Hallandale, Aventura, Golden Beach, Haulover, Sunny Isles Beach, then Bal Harbour, traveling all the way down to Miami Beach.

Reymond loved America. He was proud to have been born here, though his chronic misbehavior brought banishment to a relative's home outside Caracas. Growing up, he'd met plenty of Americans in Venezuela who lived and worked there for the oil industry. They'd always treated Reymond as one of their own, so this ride felt like a homecoming of sorts. He felt needed.

He became so lost in thought, he slammed the rear of a silver hatchback, which had stopped at a traffic light. Reymond's head kicked back, wrenching his neck, his spine rattled from so many sudden shockwaves. He gripped the steering wheel with his arms locked straight.

The hatchback skidded forward and gave Reymond a good view of the damage he'd done—crushed trunk, shattered taillights, rear window webbed with cracks, all manner of debris dropped about the street. The driver got out of the hatchback and revealed himself as the dorky businessman variety in his sports jacket and chinos. He stomped towards Reymond, fists clenched like this was the last straw to his day. He couldn't take it anymore.

The man paused when seeing the facial tattoos but recovered. He pointed at Reymond who had gotten out of his vehicle as well. "Hey, buster," the man said between his teeth, "you understand this was completely your fault, right?"

Reymond noticed a green, mesh-metal public garbage can on the curb. The can overflowed with shredded newspapers, paper bags, and food scraps, but not heavy enough to make lifting it difficult. He went to the curb and picked up the garbage can. He raised it over his head, bits of trash tumbling out. He walked the can over to the hatchback and brought it down across its front windshield, which didn't break, only suffering a long, Z-shaped scratch.

"Hey! Hey!" the man yelled. "Hey! Hey!" This was evidently his sole response to increased stress.

Reymond considered the man in a contemplative manner until raising the garbage can again. He brought it down across the windshield repeatedly. He heard a woman screaming and realized the car held a front seat, female passenger, hands over her mouth, eyes wide with terror. Why she had only now started screaming was anyone's guess.

Reymond heard sirens. He knew this couldn't possibly be the police responding to this small incident so fast, but better to be safe. He jogged back to his rental car, the front grill wrinkled but the vehicle running. The front fender appeared bent but not enough to obstruct the tires. He would outrun any police, no problem. Since his teenage years, he'd been the expert escape artist against any Venezuelan police pursuit. Their cars were fairly fast but never stood a chance against anything turbo. This wasn't what he had currently, but there was time. He could race away. No one in this solar system could catch him.

He threw the car into drive and wheeled to the right of the damaged vehicle ahead of him. Reymond floored it forward and jumped the curb. He rode over the median and mowed down an intricate arrangement of trumpet lilies.

What Reymond didn't know was that the rental car came equipped with a microchip, which allowed the nearest pursuing police officer to fire a HALT (High Speed Avoidance Using Laser Technology) laser at his car. This cut the fuel supply to Reymond's engine, and he soon rolled to a stop across two lanes of traffic. He tried repeatedly to start the car, but a trio of patrol cars came screaming from three different directions. Reymond chose to flee on foot. He made it two blocks where a gang of officers tackled him into a shrubbery block. The officers piled on afterward, all of them struggling to be the first to successfully handcuff him. It only took a few minutes.

Fourteen

Trace stopped at the Circle K and bought two coffees. He used napkins to keep the hot coffee from burning him. Meanwhile, he thought of Enrique lying in some dusty parking lot, leaking blood into a spreading pool around his slowly draining body.

When Camila opened her door, she brightened up at the sight of the coffee. She wore a black kimono waffle robe.

"What has happened to you?" she asked him. "Why are you so filthy?"

"I got into a fight. With my boss."

"Why do I keep waking up and you are gone?"

Rather than answer, he said, "My partner was killed."

"Nora?"

"No, my *detective* partner—Enrique Alvarez. He was found stabbed last night."

"Oh my God, is this connected with Nora?"

"Was Nora dating Jason Shaw? Is he the one who trafficked both of you?"

She took his hand and led him inside.

Trace looked down at himself and saw how, in the brighter light of her condo, he was far more covered in mud than he'd thought. He looked as though he'd been wrestling a bear.

Camila took the coffees from him. She used fine China cups to pour them in. She noticed him watching her. "Oh, because Styrofoam is full of chemicals. Go have a seat."

"I'm covered in mud."

"I have a cleaning service. *Es bueno.* Sit."

He went to take a tentative seat on the sofa. She came around while holding their coffees. She set them on a low, blue-tiled table.

Trace shielded his eyes, the sun overlaying the apartment in golden light. It was far too intense, and he thought of asking her to draw the shades. "Has anybody from the media called you?" he asked her. "There's an article out about some things I said. Things I shouldn't have said."

"My phone has been ringing nonstop, baby. The only person I answer to is you." She leaned forward and touched his knee. "What kind of article?"

He looked at her hand on his knee. "The other day I broke into Nora's apartment," he said. "Well, I didn't *break* in. I had a key."

"I have a key, too. Everyone does."

"I found Nora's diary."

"And you read it?"

"Some. Enough. Did he rape her?"

Camila's hands went to her face, and she inhaled. She dropped her hands in her lap. "It's not like we have a choice."

"'*We?*' You, too?"

"He has our papers, Trace! He's our only way of making money."

"When's the last time you had sex with him?"

"It wasn't by choice! You have to believe me. Nora either. The enslavement isn't over. It never is."

She went to touch him, but he spun away. He stood and walked to the window. "It *is* over with, okay? I'm taking this monster down. I think Jason Shaw might be the one who killed Nora."

"It's possible. No one will ever know, for sure. Please, let it go, all right?"

"'Let it go?'"

"*Por favor…*"

"Camila, that pretty much goes against everything I've tried to make my life about. *'Let it go?'*"

"I don't want you to end up like Nora."

"You think he did it, too."

"I know he's killed people."

"And yet you still work for him. Are you willing to repeat what you just said in a courtroom?"

"Of course not! *Dios mio,* you're scaring me."

"Nora wrote in her diary that she was scared he might kill her. Jason Shaw did it, Camila. He's the one."

"Please, baby, leave it alone. Or everyone will die."

"Don't be scared of this asshole! That's the problem. Everyone's scared of him."

"*Si*, I am terrified of him. You don't even know what you're saying."

"You no longer work for him. Is that understood?"

She half-smiled. "That is sweet. But what will I do for money, huh? How will I afford this apartment?"

Trace looked out the window at the tiny cars crossing the causeway, the tiny boats leaving V-shaped wakes, back and forth, the spiky skyline of downtown Miami, all of it presumably owned by someone. The enormity of the past two days bore down on Trace, and he felt himself trembling again. "Let me get this straight," he said. "Jason Shaw not only owns and operates that sleazy strip joint, owns property throughout Dade County, owns a South Florida restaurant chain, but he's also a murderer who secretly runs an underground sex trafficking ring."

Camila let her breath out. "It's like you were reading it from *Wikipedia*."

"Ambitious dude."

Trace noticed the glistening, crystal brandy bottle flash from the sun. Its juicy-red juiciness called to him, forced him to walk over and pour himself a glass. He downed it. He thought of Enrique. At the same morgue they'd been to themselves so many times, usually to either escort some grieving relative for identification, or to get the coroner's report from the coroner's mouth. The thought of his partner lying there on that steel table, shelved within the wall, like any other storage item, his cold body lacerated and turning gray. And Nora. What must she look like now? The formaldehyde filling their veins, changing the molecules of their tissue so bacteria found it unappetizing, at least temporarily.

Trace downed another glass of brandy, then another and another, each one slightly larger.

"Please, baby," Camila said. "He can make you disappear. He could make anyone disappear."

He gave her a somber look. "Nobody's that powerful. Fuck him. He's not the president."

He retook his seat on the couch next to her. Camila raised onto her knees and kissed the top of his head. She lay her cheek there.

His cell rang and he retrieved it from his pocket. It wasn't a number he recognized, but in light of recent events, he felt compelled to answer anyway.

"This is Reymond," the person inside the phone said. "I'm Enrique's brother. You busy?"

"Sort of. Why?"

"I'm in jail, bro. Think, you know, you could come bust me out or something?"

(Letter written by Anja Stanković, translated from Serbian.)

Baba, it's so dark where I'm writing you from I can hardly see what I'm writing. I'm in a big, dark room. I'm pretty scared.

I told our chaperone I needed to pee, and he let me come in here and I'm writing you. Light doesn't work. I can't find the toilet. Don't know how to even get this note to you. Momma was right. I was so dumb not to listen to her. This isn't a stupid modeling trip. None of these people want me to be their stupid model. PA NE MOGU DA VJERUJEM!

I kind of made friends with one of the other girls and she says she's pregnant from a client. She got rejected from another group for being pregnant, so she's with us, though she can't speak enough English to fully explain why. The ship crew tells me I'll be treasured because I'm white and blonde and beautiful. I'm a big deal. I'm going to make a lot of money.

Every girl has been forced to have sex with every crew member. I was spared since I'm being saved for The Boss. To be his new main girl basically. He prefers me unspoiled.

I would ask our chaperone how long they intend to keep us here, but they always get angry when we ask questions. Any questions. Asking for the bathroom just now almost got me beaten up.

Earlier, when I told them I wanted to go home, that got a good laugh. Looks like I'm stuck, Baba. If this is what I have to do though, then fine. Fuck it. Pay me, I guess.

Baba, please, know I can handle this, okay? No, I don't deserve getting sold like livestock to men who consider women nothing less than dutiful, praiseful receptors of their passion and mercy, but if this is where I am, and I have no have to go they're banging the doo

Fifteen

Trace waited inside a small room within the Miami-Dade Corrections and Rehabilitation Department. A pinched-mouth woman in a caged booth periodically returned the possessions of prisoners as they became released. Trace used his sixth "detective" sense to try and determine which one might be Reymond. He'd only ever met him once.

There was a thirty-something man in white, button-up shirt, pleated slacks, and expensive-looking dress shoes. He was handed back his tie, belt, and wallet. From his overnight stubble and bleary eyes, he was a DUI case. Guaranteed. Next came a young, eraser-haired youth dressed head-to-toe in *Miami Hurricanes* sportswear, obviously a marijuana case. You could still smell it on him. Next came a Hispanic man, only slightly older than Enrique with his same body category and head shape, wearing a pair of gold earrings. As the man signed the form, attesting he was being given back the entirety of his possessions, Trace made a move to shake his hand. The man was greeted by a young woman who hugged him and began sobbing. His girlfriend. Not Reymond.

Enrique had never mentioned Reymond much, only ever doing so in a hushed tone, as if fearful that speaking his name might conjure him. Enrique had once confessed that his becoming a cop was mainly a retort to his older brother and his violent habits, which were closer akin to their father's than anyone else. Likely running afoul of some local gang, their father had gone missing when Reymond was twelve, Enrique nine. Afterward, their mother sought help with a cousin who worked at the American Embassy. She helped her claim persecution so they could immigrate to the US. They lived with her sister in Hialeah while awaiting approval for asylum. In the meantime, she worked "off the books" as a housekeeper while also raising two sons who couldn't stay out of trouble. By seventeen, Reymond became such a burden he was sent back to Venezuela, meant to be raised by his uncle but was essentially on his own ever since.

Trace didn't know much else about the Alvarez Family, except there was a younger sister named Lilly somewhere, born in the U.S. Both brothers were aggressively protective of her. She attended Florida International University and studied Accounting. She'd been promised an important job in the nightclub when she graduated.

The last prisoner released was a large man, around six-foot-two, his exposed skin painstakingly inked with all manner of thorns, bleeding eyeballs, and goblins. He was the one man Trace hoped Reymond was not. Half his face was even covered in tattoos. He wore a blue mohawk. When the large man set his eyes on Trace, there was a flicker of acknowledgement, which let Trace know this was, of course, Reymond.

After getting his possessions back, which seemed to be only his wallet and a few rings, he approached Trace. He put his hand out for Trace to shake, which he did, and his hand swallowed Trace's.

"How did you know it was me?" Trace asked him.

"I remember you. We met a long time ago." To Trace's dismay, Reymond worked on clasping the rings through his nostrils, not around his fingers.

"You didn't have so many tattoos back then," Trace said.

"No, I didn't. How do we get the fuck out of here?"

Trace opened the door directly behind himself and held it open for Reymond to walk through. The two men stood together and blinked in the sunlight until Trace led him to his 4Runner, parked at a meter nearby.

"Where am I taking you?" Trace asked him. He turned to see Reymond had stopped following him about ten steps back.

"That's all right. I'll walk," he said.

"Walk where? This isn't the safest part of town."

"I don't want to, um, bother you."

"You're already bothering me. I want you to. Tell me where to take you."

"Take me to my brother's apartment?"

"You have a key?"

"Of course I do."

"Get in."

"You sure?"

"Positive. I prefer it. I have a lot I want to ask you."

Trace drove them onto I-295, crossing the causeway to Miami Beach. They rode in silence a while. Trace's questions, compounded with his confusion and grief, stayed lodged in his throat.

"Thanks for getting me out," Reymond said. "Hundred percent. I didn't know who else to call."

"You're lucky I know the only trustworthy bail bondsman in Miami."

"What was your collateral?"

"You're riding in it. How did you get my phone number?"

"My brother had given it to me for some reason. Speaking of whom…"

Trace waited but there didn't seem to be a continuation of that phrase. Reymond stared straight ahead. "Yeah?" Track asked him.

"Nothing. I forgot for a moment why I was here."

"Your brother was a dear friend of mine. More than a partner."

"Who killed him?"

"I don't know yet. Possibly a man named Jason

Shaw."

"Who's that?"

"A really bad guy."

"Why don't you arrest him?"

"I was on my way to when you called me. Why don't we go do it right now together?"

"Are you serious?"

"I might could use your help, yes."

"See, if I go, I'm probably going to kill the dude. Are you prepared for that?"

"No, we can't kill him unless he tries to kill us first."

"I can't promise you that."

"Well, you have to. We'll go to prison." Trace took a deep breath. He gripped his steering wheel harder. He gave Reymond an anxious look but threw his eyes back on the road. "Maybe I should go alone."

"Take me to my brother's apartment. I need to think about this."

"And I'd like to research and find out where Jason Shaw lives."

Off to the east, the sky darkened from banks of dark-gray clouds, stacked like filthy marshmallows. Lightning pulsed between them, the thunder like boulders tumbling. A biblical flood approached, on its way to bring savage winds and pounding rain for five minutes. Florida's topography was that it had none. It was a flat peninsula, so weather tended to speed through unimpeded.

Reymond was such a large person, his elbow kept touching Trace's. Apart from his physical presence,

Reymond also carried a psychic presence, taking up as much space and energy, if not more. He was the type of person who sucked all the oxygen out of a room. No wonder Enrique had spoken of him with such dread and reverence. Looking into Reymond's eyes was like looking into the eyes of an alligator. No soul, only hunger and an instinct derived from ruthless violence. He was polite, but it sounded forced, like he'd rehearsed the words, telling himself this was how polite people talked.

"Jason Shaw," Reymond said. "Tell me everything you know about him. Not just *'he's a really bad guy.'* I assume that. Hundred percent."

"He owns the strip club my girlfriend danced at. He owns a lot of restaurants. He's a big deal in Miami."

"You think he killed my brother?"

"I plan on asking him."

"You have proof?"

"No, but I think Jason Shaw might've also murdered my girlfriend."

"No shit. When?"

"A few days ago."

"*Puta madre.*" Reymond took this in and shook his head. "I need a shower. I smell like jail."

Bringing Reymond along to accost Jason Shaw was certainly an impromptu idea, but why not. Nothing to lose. Besides, Trace could use the extra muscle behind him. Reymond was, if anything, an imposing figure. The facial tattoo was startling, but he could make it work. Trace decided it was also best not to mention he'd been fired from the police department.

He brought the 4Runner to a stop as a railroad crossbar lowered across Biscayne Boulevard. Red lamps flashed and bells rung to herald the oncoming freight train. The rail traffic in Miami had recently increased after having shut down. This was from so many tracks getting destroyed during recent hurricanes. Now the trains seemed as though they were making up for lost time.

After the train passed, raindrops tapped the windshield, gently at first, then harder until Trace was forced to put on his wipers. He drove down I-195 to the MacArthur Causeway. He traveled beyond the freighters and cruise ships parked along the dock, each awaiting its return to the open ocean. Trace merged onto Alton Road and cut a right onto Seventeenth Street.

He found a parking space only a block away, doing a better job of parallel parking this time. Both men ducked through the rain, crossed the street, and turned right. Enrique's apartment was located inside an art deco coop, painted canary-yellow with stained glass and interlacing lines of bright blues and greens. Dwarf majesty palms marked the property lines.

Trace followed Reymond as he entered an unlocked lobby, then ascended the only available staircase. Once arriving at Enrique's door, Reymond dug a glob of keys out of his pocket. He flipped through the keys until finding the right one, trying it, but realized it wasn't the right one. He tried another and the same.

He tried three more keys, grew impatient, and smashed his right fist through one of the glass panels. He twisted his wrist down, unlatched the door from inside. Reymond opened it. He seemed oblivious to the blood coating his knuckles and dribbling down his arm and onto his right pant leg. Trace took note that Reymond had issues with impulse control.

They walked inside. The apartment was a lot tidier than Trace remembered from the few times he'd been over. Large windows allowed light to flood in, despite the storm outside, already diminishing. Enrique had added a beaded curtain to his bedroom entryway.

Trace and Enrique rarely went to each other's apartments. No specific reason. Their lives had simply kept them outdoors, especially since they both loved surfing. He spotted Enrique's shortboard hanging horizontally above the kitchen entrance, in an area that would never get too hot, so the board wouldn't warp. He heard this being explained to him in Enrique's voice and an absence ballooned within his chest. He choked and stopped himself from crying. Not in front of his brother. Smooth it out. He'd managed not to cry about any of this so far. Staying strong. Staying focused.

"What are you looking for?" Trace asked Reymond when he noticed him digging through drawers. He had wrapped a dishtowel around his bleeding hand, but it was already turning red.

"Any idea where Enrique kept his car keys?" he

asked Trace.

"Don't have those either?"

"Help me find them. It's for you. He wanted you to have his car. It was in his will."

"Enrique had a will?"

"Don't all cops have a will? You don't?"

"But you've had a probate hearing? Doesn't that take months?"

"That's bullshit. Where did you hear that?" Reymond extracted the keys from a kitchen drawer. He tossed them to Trace.

He caught them against his chest. He looked at them. "Keys to the Mustang?" he asked.

"The Mustang. Yeah, my bro wanted you to have it. Hundred percent."

"Where are the papers?"

"You'll get them."

Trace felt puny in Reymond's presence, and it began to annoy him. There was a certain level of dismissal in everything Reymond said to him, as though Trace were some inconsequential detail of a larger picture. As in, *here, have a car. Be my friend. I might need to kill you.* Plus, Reymond didn't seem too heartbroken over his brother, though he could've been the tough guy pretending. It was Trace's own excuse.

Reymond lifted a lump of glazed ceramic from a shelf. It was a brown-blue amorphous sculpture made by a child. "Look at this guy," he said. "I made this for him when we were kids. For his birthday. He still has it."

Reymond threw the ceramic sculpture against the wall, and it broke into pieces, scattering in a spray of powder. He wrapped his arms over his face and wept.

Trace wasn't sure what to do. He thought of walking over and giving the poor guy a hug but worried he might, from reflex, meet the same fate as the sculpture. Reymond soon spared him any decision by taking Trace in his immense arms and embracing him. Trace hesitated. He hugged him back, getting his own arms around him. He did his best to ignore the blood being smeared over his own shirt now. It was too late though. The hug couldn't be stopped.

Sixteen

Trace found a two-year-old phone book in a different kitchen drawer and gave it a flip-through. There were thirteen Jason Shaws. Trace found a seat on the couch while Reymond took a wicker chair, his hand wrapped in a bath towel, also turning red. He used his phone to scan social media for any clue as to Shaw's whereabouts. Though social media was often an information gold mine, they found nothing, not even a Facebook account. Google turned up several articles about Shaw's career as a renowned chef and business owner. A South Florida luxury lifestyle magazine carried a profile article with a picture of Shaw beaming at the camera, showing off his pearlies while propping his butt against a jet-black Jaguar XE. A sprawling, castle-like mansion took up the background.

Trace showed Reymond the article. "This is his

house."

Reymond squinted. "Looks like Bal Harbor to me."

"It does."

Ordinarily, as a homicide detective, Trace would've had infinite resources in this technology rich world at his fingertips, mostly from The Department of Revenue which would've given him the address on Jason Shaw's driver's license. Now, being fired, he was reduced to common social media sleuthing, like some damn teenager, and he was getting nowhere. He decided on another attempt at simply accosting Shaw at the strip club.

"Found him!" Reymond announced. "He lives in Key Biscayne. Hundred percent."

Trace couldn't hide his astonishment. "How do you know?"

"This site. I paid for a membership. '*Peeper.com*.'"

Trace ignored the embarrassment he felt at getting beat to the answer. Didn't matter. At least, they'd found him.

"If that site is as shady as it sounds," he said as a way to save face, "we'll be wasting our time. Maybe let's wait for him to leave the strip club tonight?"

Reymond shrugged. "I like the idea of surprising him at his home. I don't want to wait."

"I can dig that."

Outside it was sunny again, the streets freshly washed, the surrounding plant life sufficiently watered. The neighborhood shimmered.

Trace decided to also use this opportunity to give

the Mustang a test drive. He took Reymond to the Miami Beach Community Medical Center first to stitch up and bandage his hand. After stopping by his own apartment to change his bloodied clothing, he drove them back over the MacArthur Causeway. The engine's power was exhilarating, even as he edged through stop-and-go traffic, even as he took I-95 through downtown Miami. The car was much wider than his 4Runner, so he had to slow down when taking turns. He kept squealing the tires.

They arrived in Key Biscayne, which was a sliver of land bracketed by Crandon Park and Bill Baggs Cape Florida State Park. It was an area of Miami Trace had visited less frequently than probably any other. Never had occasion to. He didn't know anyone rich enough to live out here. He'd been to the Miami Seaquarium with a date once. Maybe the beach a couple of times. That was it.

Trace used the GPS on Reymond's phone to find Jason Shaw's address. He pulled up to the mansion's gate. He could see through the bars it was indeed the same home from the magazine article. He pressed the buzzer on the gate and a female voice responded: "Can I help you?"

"Yeah, we're here to see Jason Shaw?"

"Is he expecting you?"

"I'm Detective Trace Strickland. I was Nora's boyfriend. Tell him that."

There was a pause, then a buzzing noise as the gate slid back, allowing him to drive through. He parked next to the same Jaguar XE from the magazine picture. On the other side sat a white Lamborghini and red Corvette, both showroom shiny.

Trace sat for a moment and marveled at the size of Shaw's house. "Who is this guy?"

"Let's go ask him," Reymond said. He opened his door to get out.

They approached a round-top front door made of mahogany wood. A panel above the door contained glass of amber, blue, and pink in a geometric design. Trace estimated this foyer likely cost more than his entire apartment. He knocked.

A young woman answered. She was thin, five foot-nothing with shoulder-length black hair, straight as steel. Her eyes smiled at them from behind horn-rimmed glasses. She wore a navy-blue business jacket and pencil-skirt with black heels. She exuded a nerdy sort of sexiness.

When she invited them to come in, Trace recognized her voice as being the same from the intercom.

Trace introduced himself and Reymond. She shook their hands, and he was amazed at how firm her handshake felt. She wasn't the delicate pixie she appeared as. She introduced herself as Dara.

A giant, bearded man in a suit appeared behind them, startling them. He motioned for the two visitors to raise their hands above their heads, which they did. He frisked Reymond for weapons.

"I just got here from Venezuela," Reymond said, indignant. He brushed at his clothes, as if they'd been dirtied. "They don't allow guns on a plane. Last I heard."

"This is my brother Lionel," Dara said. "Don't mind him. Precautions are his job." She made a small laugh, as if this might ease the invasiveness of another man's hands probing them up and down their bodies. Thankfully Reymond wasn't carrying. Trace was.

When Lionel went to frisk him, Trace opened his jacket to reveal his holstered Glock. He also showed his badge. "I'm a homicide detective, and I'm not giving you my gun. You'll just have to live with that."

The bearded security guard himself carried an AR-15 semi-automatic rifle. All of them seemed to. Trace counted three other security guards. Scary stuff for home security. What kind of enemies did this Shaw guy have? Were they real?

Lionel looked to his sister who nodded. They would have to live with Trace's firearm.

Afterward, they followed Dara and Lionel into a grand hallway with Japanese wallpaper. Greek-themed images filled the friezes on the ceilings and walls. Meanwhile, a team of blue-uniformed cleaners, an equal mix of men and women, boys and girls, each used a different cleaning device. They scrubbed at what looked to be the aftermath of a particularly raucous party. Cups and bottles, many of them broken, covered the floor with streamers and latex balloons, which floated low, their helium molecules losing energy.

She motioned Trace and Reymond to have a seat on a fiberglass, chaise sofa. As Trace sat, he noticed faint cocaine residue on the table there. He noticed Dara noticing him noticing it. She motioned one of the workers over to wipe it up, which they did.

Dara smiled, unfazed. "Can I get either of you gentlemen something to drink?"

"I'm fine, thank you," Trace said.

Reymond held a finger up. "I'll take a gin and tonic."

Dara held her smile, unsure if he was serious. She gave him a curious glance. "Oookay, I'll be right back," she said.

Trace watched her go to the kitchen and wondered what her relationship to Shaw might be. He remembered Camila's statement about Shaw having sex with any of the women he wanted. Trace gripped his knees, starching himself, spring ready for whatever might happen next. He glanced at the ceiling, all the way up there. Had to be twenty feet high, maybe more.

He went to make a comment about it, but Dara was back. She held a glass of what he could only assume was an actual glass of gin and tonic. Reymond accepted it from her. He flung the contents of the glass onto the floor. Ice, alcohol, and a lone olive splattered across the tiles.

"I don't want it anymore," Reymond told her. "Go tell your boss to hurry the fuck up. We don't have all day."

She smiled wider, amused, stifling a laugh. "I'll see what I can do," she said.

Shaw was already standing there. He finished the buttons on his lapels, his hair slicked back and wet from a recent shower.

Trace and Reymond rose to their feet.

"Did I see you throw a drink on my floor?" Shaw asked Reymond, but without looking at him, still fussing over his sleeves.

"Hundred percent," Reymond said. He adjusted his clothes. They'd become bunched around his knees and elbows from sitting.

Shaw looked him up and down, nodding, offering a sideways smirk. "That's awesome. Is that your thing?" He looked at Trace and jabbed a quick thumb at Reymond. "Your buddy here, you have to watch out for this guy, huh? What a wild man."

"I'm Detective Trace Strickland," Trace said. He pulled his now illegal badge from his wallet, displaying it. "We're here to question you about the murder of Nora Montoya."

Shaw didn't flinch. "You a cop, too?" he asked Reymond. Shaw snickered. "They let you have tattoos on your face like that? You're not a cop."

"I'm not a cop," Reymond confirmed.

"He's my partner's brother," Trace put in. "He was also just murdered."

Shaw took a step back, alarmed. "The cop who got stabbed? *That's* your brother? I saw it on the news upstairs! Just right now."

Reymond nodded, frowned.

Shaw continued, "And here are the cop's brother and his partner in my very home. What do you want?"

"Nora kept a diary."

"What did she write in it? That I killed her? I *loved* that girl."

"Not as much as I did. Is that why you stabbed her?"

"I didn't do shit. I have several alibis. Check your records, detective."

"Who did you hire to do it? Was it *this* guy?" He indicated Lionel who blinked at him, bemused.

Shaw chortled. "You think I'd kill a cop? You're out of your mind."

Reymond stepped in between the two men. He faced Trace, nearly touching him with his chest. "Actually," he told him, "the questions are over. You can go home."

Trace froze, confused. "What are you talking about? Let me handle this."

Reymond walked forward against Trace's hand. "Sorry, but I only needed your help to get me in the door. I have a proposition I need to discuss with Mr. Shaw here."

"With the man who might've killed your brother? What proposition? The nightclub?"

Reymond heaved a sigh. "I know you got fired, Trace. You're not a cop anymore. My brother and me tell each other everything."

"I don't know what you're talking about," Trace said. How could Reymond have known? Fulcher had fired him *after* Enrique was murdered.

"You know exactly what I'm talking about," Reymond went on. "Drop the act."

Trace laughed from disbelief. "So you're turning on me? Sure you want to do that, Reymond? My suspension is temporary," he lied.

Reymond nodded. "Yeah, you can go get lost. I don't need you anymore."

Trace instinctively went to reach for his gun, but it wasn't called for. He backpedaled.

Shaw looked at Dara and guffawed again, incredulous. "What is going on?"

"I was lying about the car," Reymond added to Trace. "I gave it to you, so we'd be square for you bailing me out of jail. We're even now, okay?"

Trace shook his head. "You're making a gigantic mistake. Don't go into business with this scumbag. He'll take everything."

"Thanks for the ride. And for bail."

"Reymond, I'm begging you…"

"I imagine you're doing a lot of begging lately. Oh, and sorry about your chick. I know Mr. Shaw here didn't do it though. Why would he?"

"I love this guy," Shaw told Dara. "Where did you find him?"

She shook her head slow. She smirked. "He showed up. Law of attraction."

Trace remained focused on Reymond who had him

backed up to the front door. "You're going to end up getting killed." Trace told him. "Like your brother. Don't do this."

"I'm a big boy. I'll be fine. Hundred percent. Bye."

Reymond placed a large arm around Trace's shoulders while opening the front door. He pushed Trace outside. The door shut on his ass and bumped him forward. He stood there dumbfounded, grappling with the insatiable urge to about-face and kick the door in. But he couldn't. Didn't possess the authority anymore. Reymond had dead-on called him out, then threw him under the bus. What could he actually do?

He got into the Mustang and drove away, dragging his bludgeoned pride behind him. He seethed the entire way back to South Beach. He clutched the steering wheel as though he might try ripping it off. When Trace arrived home, he stormed up his stairs, entered his apartment. He went directly into the kitchen. He made himself a *Southern Comfort* on the rocks, downed it, poured another. He relished the pain this brought to his throat. He sat on his futon. He pressed his knuckles to his nose and concentrated on what to do next. Girlfriend dead. Partner dead. Job gone. His only ally turned traitor.

He lay back and fell asleep. He dreamed he was in a decrepit house. He faced a set of three bay windows, each shrouded by curtains so dusty the dust cast shadows. A little girl kneeled at his feet. She handed him dolls from a hatbox. The dolls' gold or black hair sprouted from their scalps like shave brushes. The little girl kept looking up at him, but he didn't know who she was. He asked her name several times, but she would only hand him another doll.

"What am I supposed to do with these?" he asked her. He held a mound of dolls over his lap. "I don't want them."

"You'll need them," the child said. She vanished.

Trace gazed upon adult-sized boots. They belonged to a camo-adorned man holding a machine gun. A shot rang out and the man pitched forwards. He fell across Trace's lap. Trace leapt to his feet in shock and the man slumped to the floor, and onto his back. Trace could see it was Chief Fulcher. He bent down to check his pulse and Fulcher's face changed, becoming the face of Trace's father, morphing again into his own face. The two Traces stared at one another.

His perspective ping-ponged between both Traces until the scenery spun and he awoke to a woman screaming his name. It took him a moment to understand he was back inside his apartment, and he'd been dreaming. However, the screaming continued. It was real. It was the soul-shattering scream of a woman being slowly killed. At first he thought she was in his living room but dashing there moved the voice outside. She screamed his name from the street. It was Camila.

Seventeen

The serial killer was back at the club. He admired the naked women as they danced, and he thought of how he might kill the next one. There was cause to hurry because it would be over soon. Executioners always met their executions, and his was certainly coming, expedited by the enormous blunder he'd committed last night. The Hispanic man was a cop! Shit was getting crazy. If they had surveillance footage of that cop leaving here, they likely had footage of him as well, leaving right beforehand.

Fortunate for his nerves, Camila was dancing tonight. He'd always considered her one of the better dancers. That heart-shaped face, those deep-set, brown eyes, adorable in a girl-next-door way. She was his new favorite. She looked white enough anyway. Might have to kill her though. He'd have to see. Just didn't know yet. Maybe he should stop and disappear for a while until things cooled off. Lay low.

The strip club grew crowded. News coverage of this place calling it a death magnet would seemingly have kept people away, but the opposite proved true. The Club Cabana was as busy as he'd ever seen it. The notoriety had brought curiosity seekers. Perhaps someone else would get murdered and they could watch it this time.

When Camila finished her dance, she came up to him. She pressed her body between his knees. "Did you like my dance?" she asked him. She used the same words every time, the same lilt in her voice. It was annoying. "Will you take care of me?"

He stared at her without speaking until she got the hint and went away. Didn't even seem bothered by it. She moved on to the next customer, no problem, and his mood soured more. The bartender asked him three times if he wanted a drink and he kept declining, letting his intense scowl serve as his answer. One girl after another came by and he wouldn't part with a single dollar. He stared at them until they went away.

A black-suited bouncer came over.

"What's up, my man?" he asked the serial killer. "You know the rules: They strip, you tip."

"Did you give your security tape from last night to the police?"

The bouncer looked at him askance. "Why do you ask?"

"Just wondering. Someone needs to catch this guy."

"You're here a lot, aren't you?" the bouncer asked

him. "You were here last night, too. I saw you."

The serial killer pondered what other video footage they might have. Only a matter of time until the walls truly closed in. His hands took turns kneading each other. He cracked his knuckles.

"Know what I'm thinking?" the bouncer asked him. He dented his brow, frowned. "I'm thinking it's time for you to leave, my man. Take your fake I.D. and get the fuck out."

"My pleasure," he mumbled. He got up from his stool, and he left the club. Was probably a good idea to never come back here. He didn't care.

—

He waited in his car until he spotted Camila leaving. It was after five in the morning. She looked glum, as she most always did when he saw her anywhere outside the club. Even from just the way she carried herself, he could tell she'd had an errant existence punctuated with sexual abuse and emotional neglect. She carried her beauty like a burden.

He'd been sitting in his car for nearly three hours, listening to the radio for the first hour before growing concerned about his battery draining. A few times he spotted the same bouncer come outside and look around, perhaps checking to make sure he'd left. Each time, the serial killer sank down in his seat, counted to fifty, and peeked to see the bouncer had either gone back inside or was talking to someone.

The serial killer deliberated his situation. Should he leave the city? The country? Start over somewhere with a new name? Wait until the outrage died away and resume his mission? He didn't have enough money for any of that. No choice but to stay and face the consequences, which was fine. He felt no shame for what he'd done. None of it.

He watched Camila get into a taxi. When he saw the cab stop only a block away at a red light, he started his car, backed up, and raced out of the parking lot. He pulled up behind her and saw the back of her head through the taxi's rear window. She turned her head and rubbed her eyes. The light turned green.

—

Camila lay on her hip, her right arm propped across the sidewalk. She tried getting up but kept collapsing as though pulled. She lay on her side and used her fingers to drag herself. Trace noticed the wide, dark trail she left.

He dashed downstairs and into the street. She held onto him as he pulled her to her feet. He tried walking her, but her steps came too slow, her breathing too ragged. He lifted her in his arms and carried her up to his apartment. Under more lighting, he could see how truly badly she was bleeding. They were lathered in it. Blood colored the carpet.

"Who did this?" he yelled. "Camila, tell me who did this to you!"

She closed her eyes, and Trace went insane. He shook her awake again, nearing violence.

He lifted her onto the futon, and his mind locked with indecision over whether to drive her to the hospital or call an ambulance. He decided to call an ambulance. Driving there might risk getting her triaged. Arriving by ambulance meant she'd be under medical attention already.

Trace called 911. Gave his address. Camila said his name and he felt a thud through the floor. He ran back into the living room to find she'd fallen on her face. He knelt next to her, turned her over. He held her head in his lap.

"I don't want to die," she whispered. "Don't let me die."

"Ambulance is on the way."

She closed her eyes. "Why would someone do this to me?"

"Camila, keep your eyes open. That's important, okay?"

"I'm trying."

"Did you see their face? Who attacked you?"

She swallowed hard, shook her head. "He was young."

"Camila, seriously, open your eyes."

"He was a regular," she said. "At the club." She turned her head away and he steered it back.

"Camila, stay with me…Come on."

She closed her eyes, and he patted her cheeks until her eyes reopened.

He heard sirens far off, the lonely lament of healers rushing through the night, an utterly nerve-wracking tune.

145

Eighteen

Trace wore his badge outside his jacket, a strip of black tape stuck horizontally across the front, the look on his face daring anyone to tell him he couldn't wear it. All police officers wore black tape when attending a downed officer's funeral.

Enrique's funeral was held at St. Joseph's Catholic Church in the town of Surfside, south of Bal Harbour. Stain glassed windows radiated out from the church's center like unfolding rose petals.

Earlier that day, Trace had visited coroner Jesus Gonzales, finding out Enrique had suffered death by "exsanguination due to multiple stab wounds." He also learned the Department Chaplain and Cemetery Officer ended up making the funeral arrangements. The reason why the funeral felt so rushed was because it was—a combination between Enrique's family wanting to get it over with, and Fulcher wanting to keep the story in the headlines before it got buried and people moved on with their lives. Still, it felt odd to be attending Enrique's funeral before Nora's.

Trace had phoned the chaplain himself and offered to serve as a color guard or usher. Instead he was made a pallbearer with Reymond and four cousins. When Trace spotted Reymond at the funeral, he cocked his finger at Trace and winked. He turned to receive a hug from someone.

As Trace was about to take his seat, mid-pew, Callaway and Paletti found him.

"How are you holding up, buddy?" Paletti asked him. His thinning hair glistened with sweat.

Trace plunged his hands in his pockets and addressed the floor. "I'll be okay."

"People are dropping all around you," Callaway said. "That's a rough deal."

Trace brought his eyes up. "What is that supposed to mean?"

"Easy, easy," Paletti patted both of them on their chests. "We're at a funeral, guys."

"You know I've done nothing wrong," Trace said. "Stop making things worse for me."

"People are dropping all around you," Callaway repeated, too big of an asshole to keep his voice down or watch his words. "I'm certainly glad you're not *my* friend. Otherwise, I might be the next stiff lying in a box, huh?"

Paletti nudged his chin at the podium. "You going to say anything up there today?" he asked Trace.

He took this chance to finish having his seat. He

crossed his arms. "Nope."

"Wasn't he your partner?"

"Leave me alone."

"If I get killed will you give a speech at my funeral?" Paletti asked Callaway.

Callaway tsked and grinned. "I'll dance maybe!"

The two detectives laughed loud but caught themselves. Trace almost wanted to turn around so he could count the offended faces. He didn't have to. Callaway and Paletti pouted and slinked away. Trace realized he'd never mentioned finding Nora's diary to them but watched them leave anyway. He could no longer stomach the thought of them getting to take down Shaw, should the notion ever strike them. Trace deserved to be the one. Not them. Never them.

Trace noticed a young woman who reminded him of Camila. He had visited Camila in the ICU prior to the funeral, but she never woke up during his visit. For fifteen minutes, he'd sat there and stared at the pale shell of a person he'd once made love to, now completely unmoving and breathing with the help of an endotracheal tube down her throat.

Desperate to lose the image from his mind, Trace surveyed the crowd behind him. He spotted an elderly woman in a black dress with stockings and a veil. Enrique's mother. He'd met her a few times at Enrique's birthday parties. A friendly enough woman but quiet. And tiny, so diminutive it was impossible to believe the tough things he'd heard about her. The immigrant who had found a new life for herself and her family despite every circumstance in the world going against her.

Trace had indeed been offered the chance to give a eulogy based on his "close personal friendship" with Enrique, but he'd declined. He couldn't go through with it. Not with everything else happening. Too afraid that standing before the eyes of so many people might melt him. Though he realized this move would be criticized, he couldn't bring himself to care. He had nothing left to give anyone.

Though Enrique hadn't been killed in the line of duty, he was given full military-style honors regardless. The funeral started with the police chaplain making a speech and acknowledging the somber, tragic nature of this gathering. He mentioned *Matthew 5:4*, blessing those who mourned, "for they will be comforted." God would always make everything better, though Trace wondered why this couldn't have been done without anyone dying over it.

The next speaker was Reymond, dressed in a black suit too tight for him, his bandaged hand, although fresh and white earlier, was now unraveling and sponged with blood. A surprised murmur rippled through the congregation. He approached the podium and unfolded a piece of paper from his pocket.

"To the people who knew my brother," Reymond said. He cleared his throat to keep speaking, "there are no words that will give us the comfort we seek. All we can do is pledge our undying thirst for revenge." He paused for effect. A few men grunted approval, but it was nowhere near the reaction Reymond seemed to anticipate. He frowned with his brows puckered. "I will vow right here and right now that I'm going to get the piece of shit who did this. For those of us who knew my brother as I did, our pain is raw and it's bleeding. We say to ourselves, if we could've had one more minute to say goodbye, to let him know how much we loved him. But were we given that chance? No, we were not. So the only action left to take is to honor Enrique by remembering his legacy. And murdering without mercy whoever did this. They deserve death!

"Today we say goodbye to my little brother Detective Enrique Alvarez, to pay respect to his service and sacrifice. God bless you, my dear, little brother. May you rest in peace. May your enemies suffer at the altar of vengeance. We will bring you their blood! We will drink their blood together for the Gods of Rock and Roll! *Hallelujah!*"

The church remained completely silent, save for the occasional sniffle or cough. If anyone was shocked or outraged by Reymond's eulogy, they didn't dare voice it. He left the podium and walked to the front pew, opposite side from Trace. Reymond and his mother exchanged glances. He sat next to the young woman who had reminded Trace of Camila. He recognized her as the sister. She wore a black dress with a black pill hat. She stared empty-eyed at her brother's casket. Reymond placed his arm around her and whispered into her ear, but her expression stayed unaffected.

Before the next speaker could take the stage, Trace stood and jogged to the podium. He looked out across the congregation, saw everyone looking back, none of them realizing he wasn't a planned eulogist. He took a deep breath and fought the urge to go sit back down again.

"Some would say that what we do in our profession is a calling," Trace's voice cracked, and he coughed. He focused on the blank surface of the podium. "This job attracts those who truly believe they can make a difference. That's why it attracted me anyway. I – *'we'* —we in this room could not imagine ever doing anything else. I know Enrique couldn't. Though we face the unknown when we go to work every day, we accept this danger. Enrique was my partner for twelve years and he helped me out of more danger-ous situations than I could count. We always had each other's back. This tragedy, his death, is so diffi-cult for any of us to comprehend. Why him, you know? Of all people.

"The huge turnout today is not only a tribute to his service, but an acknowledgment of the amazing per-son he was. It's a testament to the impact he had on families, on his friends, the community. See, Enrique was more than just my partner...or my surfing buddy. He was a true friend and a good soul. The wounds caused by his death will never completely heal for me and the void he leaves will never be filled. And...and I guess that's all I have to say. I don't know. Thank you."

He went and sat back down. He stayed there, awkward and stiff, waiting for the funeral director or someone to let him know when it was time to help move the casket, so he could get the hell out of there.

—

He met Chief Fulcher in the reception room. Fulcher still had a black eye, which made it impossible for Trace to look at his face for more than a second. They stood next to a framed painting of Jesus, suffering rather horrifically, his eyes rolled heavenward.

"Liked your speech," Fulcher told Trace.

"Thanks. Just came out of me."

Fulcher looked him up and down, nodded. "It was needed after his brother got up there. What a fucking idiot. That's him, huh?"

"You never met him? Thought you were going into business with this guy."

Fulcher winced. "Not anymore. He's partnering with Jason Shaw now. I can't do business with fucking Jason Shaw."

"They're going to be partners? Shaw said yes?"

"It's a prime location. He'd be crazy not to." Fulcher worked his lips together and patted Trace's arm. "Look, I'm going to reinstate you."

"My speech was that good?"

"That and we do need your help. I shouldn't have fired you. I was angry about Enrique."

"Me too."

"I know." Fulcher rested a hand on Trace's shoulder, bore into his eyes, like he wanted to say more. He patted his arm again and stepped back. "I know you are."

Trace glanced at Fulcher's face and his eyes once more went straight to the bulging, indigo bruise surrounding his eye. "Thanks," Trace said. "Means a lot to me. Means everything."

"That's good to hear," Fulcher told him. "That's good."

After the funeral, a procession of eighty vehicles wound its way towards Caballero Rivero Woodlawn North in Little Havana. This was a mere five blocks from where Enrique had grown up in his family's first American home.

(Letter written by Anja Stanković, translated from Serbian.)

Don't have too much time, Baba. I tried calling you. My fingers tremble with so much anger that it's hard for me to write. One of the girls got beat up really bad for not doing something that one of our chaperones wanted her to do. Some degrading, sexual act. They assault these girls nightly. This one guy went too far though and she won't wake up. She's in the infirmary with a broken nose, broken cheekbone, broken ribs, and who knows what else. Her poor face is destroyed. Never witnessed anything more horrible or violent in-person in my life.

One of the girls told me that, before even getting put on this ship, they'd been herded to an auction where they were stripped naked and paraded onto a stage. They were sold to the highest bidder. Can you believe this happens?

I'm in a group with four other girls. Two of them are Chinese, one is from Malaysia, and another from Pakistan. They seem to all be around 15 or 16. I'm the oldest by at least 2 years! We were each fooled by the same "Become a Fashion Model in the US!" ads. They're very pretty and sexy enough to be real models, and it's a horror what they're being forced to do instead. Sooner or later, it will be my turn, I guess. I'm lucky I have them to prepare me.

Baba, I'll look for a private place to call you again. I'm still being saved for "The Boss," and I'm not hearing the greatest things about him. I'm hoping it's only exaggeration because they're jealous. The ship crew don't hide their hatred for me, often spitting at my feet and laughing about it. You would think the other girls would hate me more, but they don't. They're always offering me to hang out with them. Have a few drinks. I'm not sure how I would treat another woman being treated so preferentially over me, but I doubt I'd want to give her my booze.

Anyway, we should arrive in Miami tomorrow. Not sure how you'll get this letter or any of them but still feels good to write this down to someone. Write down what's happening.

Tell Momma I tried calling her, but she didn't answer. I wish somebody would answer.

Nineteen

Lying nude in a lounge chair, only a few feet from his eastern swimming pool, Shaw drank a beer at ten in the morning. He considered everything he had to do that day, none of it more important than the shipment tonight. He decided to scratch the rest till tomorrow.

He'd been in the trafficking business less than a couple years, first initiated by the Chinese organization *Mei-Yu*. They were the previous owners of The Club Cabana Strip Club, forced to sell because of "visa issues." Shaw was reluctant at first. He felt sorry for these girls being forced to sleep with such gross filth sometimes. It was horrible. However, his misgivings were soon replaced by dollar signs. A few more years of this and he estimated he would own the entire state of Florida.

There were hurdles. Despite being an expert at converting money lines into implied probabilities, he was on a major losing streak. His online gambling had become a drain. Despite a recent, morbid surge, The Club Cabana wasn't making the money it once did. Some of his restaurants were even going under, a casualty of oversold, overpriced property in an oversaturated market. Jason Shaw was hemorrhaging money. This shipment of new girls was arriving in the nick of time.

The twins Dara and Lionel approached him, neither reacting to his nudity, both fully accustomed to it. Dara clutched a leather-bound presentation folder housing the investor contracts. Reymond and Chief Fulcher were due to arrive any minute.

"What's on your mind?" he asked Dara.

"Why are you bothering with this loser?"

"It's beachside property on South Beach, my dear. Do you understand how seldom that comes along?"

"I looked at your books this morning. You can't afford it."

He clicked his tongue, scratched his chin. "I can't afford *not* to buy this place. Beachside property."

"This Reymond guy is unhinged. He has a record."

"He's fine. The Miami Beach Police Chief is an investor, too. We're protected."

"That sounds like an *equation* for disaster to me." She sat on the lounge chair next to him, her knees pressed together. She folded her hands on them. "You're being reckless."

"Stop talking like my mother." He noticed Lionel standing there. "Lionel, have a seat. Quit standing there like a statue."

Lionel went to a nearby table and sat on one of the four chairs surrounding it. He remained looking down at Shaw, Lionel's shades too small for his head. Though naturally his face appeared larger than when he was younger, it was the same face. To Shaw, he looked like a large boy with a neck beard, which was why he would always see the beard as silly.

Shaw had met the siblings when they were scrawny, homeless kids which his security staff had caught jumping his fence. Dara and Lionel had recently escaped from the Florida Charity Children's Home. This was back when Shaw lived in Coral Gables. The twins had planned to sneak in through a window and steal some food, assuming they were less likely to be noticed in a huge house. On surveillance he'd found Dara appealing and asked that both be brought to him, though he dismissed his attraction upon seeing she was a minor. He still noticed an intelligence there, a cunning. He also adored her brother. He appeared oafish, but Shaw could see he was fiercely loyal. Anyway, Shaw couldn't help himself. He had a soft spot for castaways. He let them stay. He gave them jobs.

Dara became his full-time personal assistant. She was meticulous and fussy, which was to say, the female version of him. She soon grew into the elegant, young woman he saw before him.

"Can you at least change the name of the club?" she was asking him.

"Why? I love the name!"

"'*Sweet Demon Love Baby*?' What does that even mean?"

"It means whatever people want it to mean."

"That's what's called a '*marketing challenge*.'"

"With a location like that, we could call the place 'Ugly, Steaming Shithole' and people would show up. And with the menu I have in mind? Forget it. Wait, what time is it?"

She checked her watch. "They were supposed to be here ten minutes ago."

"Someone should check the front door then. Lionel?"

Lionel nodded and moved to go inside the mansion. Another security guard followed him in. Shaw employed four of these guards during the day, but a different four at night, each working twelve-hour shifts with no days off. They were paid above normal scale and given the run of the house, so this normally wasn't an issue. Shaw's only qualification for them was to possess a firearm license. It was Lionel's job to conduct a background check, though Shaw often doubted how thorough of a job he did. Didn't matter though. Shaw valued loyalty above a clean background.

Dara hugged the folder to her chest. "You know I would never dare tell you what to do, Shaw, but--"

"Yo! Yo! Yo!"

Shaw turned at the voice. It belonged to Reymond, who wore a cream-colored guayabera with cotton slacks and loafers. Lionel marched behind him, arms crossed, concerned, a protective stance.

"You're fucking *naked*, dude." Reymond noted. "What the fuck."

"You have a keen sense for the obvious. Have a seat." He used his foot to indicate by "seat" he meant the space at the foot of his lounge chair.

"I'm not sitting there! Are you crazy? Trying to play with my head, huh? Psyche me out or something?"

"Dara has the contracts ready. Where's Chief Fulcher?"

Reymond shifted on his heels. "Yeah, Chief's out of the picture."

"Why's that?"

Reymond rolled his head, loosening it. "Whatever, bro. We don't need him. Let's see those contracts."

"But Chief Fulcher's name is on these contracts. I'll have to do new ones."

"Scratch his name out. Fuck it. I don't want to wait. Look, he doesn't want to be involved without my brother. He's pretty shaken up about him."

"Aren't you?"

"Of course! I just came from his funeral. But business is business, right? I have my entire life savings in this place. I don't want to lose my brother *and* my livelihood, too."

"What did you do to your hand? Been meaning to ask you."

Reymond looked at his hand, freshly bandaged. "I was jerking off. Can I, please, see the contracts, please?"

Shaw looked at Dara, still sitting. She handed Reymond the folder and a pen. He took the folder but waved off the pen. "I have my own," he said. He took a pen from inside his jacket and read the contract. He moved his lips while he read.

"This says you're giving me 'preferred shares?'" Reymond asked. "Gives you a lot of control over everything, doesn't it? The bar and the restaurant, too?"

Shaw searched the ground around him for the bottle opener. He located it and used it to open another beer. "Sure does," he answered. He held the bottle up. "Beer?"

Reymond stayed locked on the contract. "And this says you're making your investment in the form of *'Debt Securities with Warrants.'* What does that mean?"

Dara spoke up, "Means Mr. Shaw gets paid as a portion of the overall revenue, regardless of the profit."

"So…I pay you a monthly fee, no matter what? Even if I'm not making money?"

"That is correct," Shaw answered.

"How the hell am I supposed to do that? Takes at least a year for any food business to make a profit. Any dummy knows that."

"And ninety-five percent of them fail. Were you not aware of this?"

"If I had that kind of money, what would I need *you* for?"

Shaw sat up, shielded his eyes. "Is there a problem?"

Reymond pointed at a different page. "And it says here, if I die that you get full ownership of the place? What is *this* bullshit?"

"Sign it, Reymond. Or get the hell out of here."

Reymond threw down the contract. The papers fluttered, some of them looping dangerously close to the pool. Dara leaped to her feet and ran around. She collected whichever pages didn't blow away from her.

"I see what's going on here," Reymond said. "You've decided I'm a complete moron. Hundred percent. I'm not signing this."

"But you are though," Shaw said.

Seemingly knowing a cue when he heard one, Lionel removed a .44 Magnum revolver from his jacket. He steadied it at Reymond's face.

Reymond chuckled. "You want me to sign this bullshit contract or else you'll shoot me?"

"How's that liquor license coming?"

"Um, I'll need at least six months."

"You have three days. I like you, Reymond. I dig that fucked-up tattoo on your face. Coming into my home, tossing your drink on the floor. I loved that shit. You're a mad man." Shaw stood and came closer to Reymond, coming almost chest-to-chest with him, savoring how uncomfortable it must've made this machismo dickhead feel to be this close to a naked man. "But if you thought I was going to write you a big, fat check just because I admired the size of your balls, then, yeah, I might actually be judging you to be a complete moron."

Reymond backed up. He scrutinized everyone until his sight ended on the gun barrel pointed at him. He motioned for Dara to give him the contracts, now grass-stained and wrinkled but fully collected. "Fine. I'll sign. I had some questions. That's all. I can't have questions sometimes?"

"Nope."

Reymond took a few more steps back. He gave Shaw a troubled look, but he signed the papers. He handed them back, almost dropping them again.

"How about we take a trip?" he offered. "Check the place out? I have a lot of ideas I want to talk to you about."

"I'd like that, yeah. Tonight. I have something I want to show you too. Dara, give him the address to the warehouse."

"The warehouse?"

"Yeah, where we're picking up my shipment to-night. *The* shipment."

Shaw didn't have to turn his head to know Dara was looking at him as if he'd lost his mind. Maybe he had. He didn't care. He was having fun. Reymond was fun.

Twenty

Trace drove the Mustang to Fulcher's home in Hollywood. The chief of police's house was a touch quainter than he'd expected, though he couldn't have said what he'd expected exactly. He brought flowers, which he'd purchased from a traffic light vendor on US1. The highway traced the east coast from Miami to southern Broward.

He knocked on the front door and was greeted by Esther, Fulcher's wife. She greeted Trace with enthusiasm while he took off his shoes without request, simply judging he was meant to from the collection of boots, sandals, and sneakers by the door. Fulcher entered the foyer and Trace cringed to see his black-eye was worse, much darker and distended. He gave Trace a warm handshake and welcomed him, thanked him for accepting his dinner invite. Out of nervousness Trace gave the flowers to Fulcher's wife, nearly skewering her face with them.

Fulcher went to the stairs on the left and took a few steps. He shouted a series of names, which Trace attempted to remember—Lucy, Wally, and Todd. He'd never met Fulcher's kids and had forgotten he had any until this moment. It was hard to imagine his boss as someone who participated in such derivative exercises as having kids, but here they came as a collective clumping of steps descending the stairs. Soon Trace was confronted with a trio of teenagers. He was introduced to each one and he shook their hands in turn, though he wouldn't get a good look at any of them until seated at the dining room table.

The youngest was Fulcher's daughter Lucy, a sallow-skinned, rake-thin girl, her angular face framed by twin sheets of black hair. A tiny hoop ring pierced her left nostril while her ears held their own assemblage of hoops. She wore a black Marilyn Manson T-shirt, large enough to double as a dress.

Wally was the middle child, a blonde, athletic-type, judging from his muscular build. He wore a yellow and orange, collared shirt with ripped jeans. The oldest was Todd, brown-haired with an odd, porno mustache like a goatee but without the chin section. He was dressed similarly to his brother but choosing shorts instead of jeans. He also had a black eye, identical to his father's, and Trace couldn't help but double-take when he noticed it. He chose not to mention it, though he would worry about the black eye's origin throughout the meal.

Esther inserted Trace's flowers into a vase and

made them the centerpiece for the dinner table as everyone found their chair. The kids sat on one side while Trace was relegated to the other, alone between two empty chairs. Fulcher and his wife sat at either end. The course for the evening was lasagna, though she'd replaced ground meat with ground chicken. Trace found it delicious actually.

Conversation came stilted as everyone adapted to one another's presence. Trace sensed the occasion of Fulcher's family sitting down together for dinner was an anomaly reserved for him. He felt sure Fulcher likely had never once invited any other police detective over for any reason, let alone dinner. No one seemed sure of how to behave or what to talk about.

After finishing half his plate, Fulcher rested his elbows on the table and laced his fingers together. "I want you to stay on this sonofabitch Shaw," he said to Trace. "He's tied in with your woman's murder. I don't know how, but I feel it. He's been a cancer on this city for too long."

Fulcher's family looked up at this, suddenly and rapturously interested. His father had not only invited a police detective to dinner, but one whose "woman was murdered?" Astonished the chief would open such a confidential subject in front of his family, Trace felt a wave of prickly heat wash over his back. Self-consciousness. Trace took a moment to wipe his mouth with a cloth napkin while he decided on what to respond with. "What about Callaway and Paletti?" he asked.

"They'll remain on the case. You'll help them."

"I don't think they like me."

"They're pissed you didn't turn out to be the murderer. They thought they had this wrapped easy. Now your innocence means more work."

Trace was relieved to learn of his innocence. He wasn't sure where he stood with the chief exactly, only that matters had improved since the funeral. The dinner invitation was also a great sign, but to hear it verbalized lifted tons off his shoulders. He knew Callaway and Paletti had visited Camila and, though she'd given a hazy description of her attacker, it became fairly clear it wasn't Trace.

The middle child Wally scooted forward in his chair. He hadn't touched his food yet. "Is Jason Shaw that guy who owns that strip club where the strippers keep getting killed?"

Fulcher flapped a hand at him. "Be quiet."

"I'm just asking!" he whined.

Fulcher's wife Esther laughed, a nervous titter. "Wally, I'm not going to ask how you know a single thing about any strip club."

"Trace here was dating one of the dancers who got murdered," Fulcher explained to his son. "There was some slight suspicion over poor Mr. Strickland here, but another dancer got attacked and she says Trace didn't do it."

Again, Trace felt stupefied at hearing Fulcher discuss an open investigation in the full presence of his family. Was this normal? Was his family also aware it was Trace who'd given Fulcher the black eye? *Get a good look at the man who attacked your father, kids.* His children's attention on Trace became laser-centered, making Trace feel as though he might prefer spending the rest of his visit under the table. *And Chief was upset with me for talking to a reporter?*

"I think it would be a good idea for you to shadow this man," Fulcher continued. "Follow up with what he's doing exactly. Every minute."

"Won't be easy. He employs a lot of people whose only purpose in living is to protect him."

"Keep an eye out on Enrique's brother too. I don't trust Venezuelans."

"You didn't trust Enrique?"

"Enrique's different. He's more like one of us."

Wally piped up, his mouth full. "American?"

Fulcher ignored his son, still talking to Trace: "Look, I invited you over here for dinner because I felt bad for you. I know you're going through a difficult time. I want to help you, but…" Fulcher trailed off while cutting into a square of lasagna. "You worry me, Trace," he said eventually, not looking up from his plate. "You're too soft. Too nice. I like my detectives to be a lot tougher."

"Apologies if I've let you down somehow," Trace said, louder than he meant to. "I know men in our field have to be tough, but we also have to relate and empathize, don't we, sir?"

Fulcher's daughter snorted. "Ha! He called you 'sir.'"

"I'm saying, 'Don't be a pussy.'" Fulcher paused after seeing his wife flinch at the P-word. He continued, unbothered. "Go after this Reymond guy, too. He seems like the type who would kill his own brother. South Americans are ruthless. Don't rule out *anyone*."

"Is this why you're backing out of the nightclub?"

This was apparently news to his children. It even caused a brief uproar with Lucy and Todd. They protested hard. They'd apparently been enthused about their father being partners in a nightclub and the social perks this could win them. They implored him for answers. Wally pouted but kept quiet.

Fulcher ignored his children until his oldest Todd shook his head. He sucked his cheeks in, unaccepting of his father's dismissal. "I heard he's the best chef in the world," Todd said. "He's a cook who's a crook?"

"That's a way to put it."

"Why would someone with as much money as Jason Shaw need to be corrupt?"

"Because people with lots of money live in constant fear of losing it," Fulcher answered his son. "Too much is never enough for these people." He turned his attention back to Trace again. "Come by my office tomorrow morning, first thing. I'll give you back your badge."

Trace agreed to do so because he didn't have the nerve to remind the chief he'd never gotten around to *taking* his badge. "Thanks," he muttered.

"Care for some wine?"

Wine would've been wonderful. Trace opened his

mouth in agreement to one glass but stopped himself. No more drinking. Not until he got to the bottom of everything. Would one glass hurt though? Wouldn't it be awkward to turn down his boss after discussing his reinstatement? Trace flipflopped a hundred more times within the span of a few seconds, then said: "No thank you."

"I want some wine!" Fulcher's daughter and older son shouted, more or less in unison.

"May I be excused?" asked Wally, the blonde middle child.

A side light from over the table caught Todd's face and altered its shadows. Trace experienced a revelation of having seen Todd somewhere. The Club Cabana! During one of the rare occasions he'd visited Nora at work. She pointed him out as a creep and Trace made sure to keep that face in mind, which was not hard since the guy looked so young.

"I should go get busy," Trace said. He scooted his chair back and stood. He told his boss' children that it had been a pleasure to meet them, which was the truth. It was enlightening. He thanked Chief Fulcher for inviting him to dinner, for introducing him to his wonderful family, and for giving him a second chance. He would never forget it. He also thanked Esther for welcoming him into their home. He thanked her for an amazing dinner. Jason Shaw, eat your heart out.

Twenty-One

Shaw drove the Lamborghini down I-95. It was the least favorite of his cars, but the new girls always respected it. Put them at ease to know the man who owned them had at least paid plenty. The problem with such a sports car was its awful visibility. Tight parking could be a logistical nightmare. The car was simply too loud and impractically designed. There was barely trunk space for a backpack.

Dara rode in the passenger seat. He always brought her along to meet the new girls since it helped to have another female there, putting them more at ease, disillusioning as that later became. Dara abhorred this task, hyper-aware of the inherent betrayal she felt from these other females.

His car phone sang the opening notes of "Back in Black," an old AC/DC anthem. Shaw pressed a button, and the caller was on speaker.

"Mr. Shaw," Charles, his bookie.

"Yessir," Shaw answered. He pulled off the inter-state and into the Miami Design District, a formerly forgotten warehouse neighborhood north of down-town. "How much money did we win on Sunday?" he asked.

A pause. "Are you kidding?"

"You ask that in a deadly serious tone. That bad?"

"Awful. And you haven't paid these people for what you already owe them."

"Charlie, what happened? Why do we keep los-ing?"

"Shaw, I set odds, I place bets, and I pay out win-nings on behalf of other people. That's the extent of my job, baby. I don't guarantee nothing."

"Wait—How much did we lose?"

"Quarter-mil."

Shaw heard Dara gasp and shift in her seat. She straightened herself. "God…"

He veered into the left lane, a maneuver met with a chorus of car horns behind them.

Charles must have heard the commotion. "Shaw, you there? What happened?"

"I'm going to kill you."

"Calm down. I'm the only reason these people ha-ven't gotten revenge on you yet."

"You lose a quarter-million of my money and now you're threatening me? Where are you? Tell me. This moment. Because I'm coming there to hurt you. Like *hospital*-hurt you."

"Far as we go back together, this is how I get

treated, huh?"

Shaw realized Dara was touching his arm, and he calmed down. "Who told you to bet that much of my money?"

"You did," Charles said.

Dara pulled on Shaw's elbow. "Call him later when you're not driving. You need to get yourself under control."

More out of frustration than obedience, Shaw pressed the button to end the call.

He drove for a while in silence, fuming. This seemed to make Dara nervous because she kept crossing and uncrossing her legs.

"What was I telling you this morning?" she asked him.

"There's some scam behind this. I'm getting ripped off."

"You're going to miss our turn. It's right there." She pointed.

He slowed down to take the corner. He made a right onto NE 40th Street, placing them right in the heart of the Design District. Once a commercial dead zone, the district had become a tourist mecca of fancy art galleries and high-end fashion stores with the oc-casional antiques dealer. However, the district fringes remained mostly rusted warehouses, which was where Shaw kept his.

"I still cannot believe you invited that buffoon to come here," Dara said.

"Reymond's fine. I want to give one of these girls to

him for the night. As a peace offering. Make him feel good."

"I'm sure he'll oblige. He's disgusting."

"I'm thinking of keeping one of these girls privately just for me. There's one who's supposed to be super beautiful. A Serbian."

"You cannot afford that, Shaw. She needs to work."

"You sound jealous."

"What if she doesn't like you back?"

"She'll learn to."

Another two blocks and a left turn and Shaw pulled into a small, oblong parking lot next to his warehouse. He sent a text to his man: *We're here. U?*

The warehouse stood suffocated in darkness and multiple layers of graffiti. It was three stories tall, wrapped in old aluminum, rusted at the corners. Missing panels of higher sidewall promised a large and empty space within. Lionel already sat parked there in the black passenger van, which would transport the girls back to his mansion. Lionel waved at him.

"When will the girls be here?" Dara asked. "I hate this."

As if in answer, Shaw got a text in reply: *"5 min."*

(Note written by Anja Stanković, translated from Serbian.)

The Rules:

Health will be tested weekly.

Always use condoms, always.

The Boss' word is law. Do not test him!

Get money immediately after client enters your room.

If client becomes abusive, yell for help unless client is VIP.

Do not allow client to sleep in your room! If client falls asleep, alert an assistant.

No toys or animals allowed unless cleared by the Boss.

No urination or defecation allowed by either yourself or the client as part of service.

Twenty-Two

After leaving Fulcher's house, Trace drove directly to visit Camila again at Mount Sinai Medical Center. He received conflicting information as to her current accommodations but found her recently relocated in the third floor ICU. She looked precisely as he'd left her, stone still in her bed, the covers pulled to her neck, presumably to hide her bandages. As earlier, no one else was there. He wasn't sure what to make of this. Where were her friends?

Her bed tilted, so her feet lay elevated above her stab wounds, which were elevated above her heart. Kept the blood flowing in a healthy direction. Her face remained pale, waxen almost. Her small lips, normally so red and ripe, were now white and scaly. No one had bothered to remove her fake lashes, so they were heavy with dust.

A nurse came into the room, and Trace averted his eyes as the nurse checked Camila's bandages for cleanliness and her stab wounds for infection. Though Trace hadn't asked, the nurse informed him they would likely be holding her for at least ten days after her "selective nonoperative management."

He asked her if he could borrow a pen, and the nurse gave him a ballpoint from her pocket, nonchalantly as though she did this her entire day. He stayed for another twenty minutes after the nurse had left without asking for her pen back. He placed Camila's flowers on her nightstand and wrote her a note on the blank card, which had come with the flowers. Trace wrote: "*Sorry I'm not here. I'm out trying to find him, the guy who did this.*" He considered elaborating on who he meant by "the guy," but it was a dumb flower note. He realized what he'd written was too coarse for such a note in the first place. He scratched out his message and opted for drawing a small heart with the message: "*Please get better. I need you! – Trace.*"

Combined with his messy scratch-outs, his new message looked aesthetically obscene. He checked around for something else to write on but came up empty. This hideous note would have to do.

He next drove the Mustang to Enrique's apartment. Though Fulcher had stressed he shadow Jason Shaw, Trace felt the easier target was Reymond. At least, initially. Shaw was too protected. He had a hunch Reymond would lead him to Shaw anyway.

While driving there, Trace considered switching vehicles since Reymond was too likely to recognize this car. The 4Runner blended in with the other traffic better. Nevertheless, Trace needed Reymond to sign over the papers if he truly intended for Trace to have his brother's old car. Could make for a halfway decent excuse in case Reymond caught him tailing. Trace took the Mustang.

He double-parked a block away from Enrique's apartment on Twelfth Street. There were no spaces available for him to park properly. Also, he had to be ready to follow at a discreet distance the instant he spotted Reymond. As a hiding tactic, Trace sat parked on the opposite side of the street. He faced away from Enrique's building, monitoring it through his side and rearview mirrors.

After two hours and no sign of him, Trace grew worried that perhaps Reymond had elected to get a hotel room, so he could avoid such a situation as this. Worse yet, he could be staying with Shaw. He considered driving to Key Biscayne and waiting somewhere hidden outside Shaw's estate.

Trace's cellphone rang. He didn't recognize the number but answered anyway.

"Hey," a female voice said. "This is Janis Brown. The reporter? I visited you at your apartment the other morning."

"Looking to write a follow-up story? Maybe this one will be worse."

"I'm sorry about that. It's why I'm calling. To apologize. My editor got carried away."

"Uh-huh, and you had nothing to do with it."

"Not nothing…I'm not that kind of reporter, okay?"

"Whatever. It's done."

"Did you hate my article that much?"

"Haven't brought myself to read it honestly. Kind of in the middle of something."

"Is there a chance I could interview you again? Maybe I could help you clear up your image this time."

"My image is fine. Stop bothering it."

"Let's at least meet up and discuss it? Tomorrow morning?"

"I don't think so."

"I'll bring the coffee," she added. "Or we could meet up tonight? Is tonight better? "

He was about to hang up on her when he spotted Reymond crossing the street in front of him. Trace froze, convinced he now sat face-to-face with him, but Reymond resumed walking without reaction. Trace figured he must have parked far away enough. Or Reymond's mind was already on where he was going. Yet Trace was so close. How did he not see him? Reymond took keys out and unlocked some type of teal-colored SUV, parked on the same side of the street as Trace, about a dozen cars up. Another rental.

"Meet me at *Sweet Demon Love Baby*," Trace said to Janis Brown, the reporter. "Let's say eleven. It's where the Avalon Night Club used to be." And the most neutral meeting spot he could think of. She couldn't accuse him of being naked this time. He'd been meaning to snoop around the nightclub anyway. See what clues he might find. He ended the call.

Reymond started his car and eased into the road. Trace waited for him to reach the nearest traffic light before cranking the Mustang and pulling out as well. He made sure not to get too close. He hoped another car might turn and fill in the gap between them but no such luck. Trace found himself directly behind Reymond and became convinced he would recognize the sound of the Mustang's engine. The aluminum cylinder heads, with its semi-hemispherical combustion chamber, made a chugging, growling noise which was unmistakable.

The light changed green, and Reymond shot forward. Trace managed to keep a discreet distance as he followed him up Fifth Avenue, across the McArthur Causeway, and onto I-95. He assumed he was headed either to Shaw's estate or to *Sweet Demon Love Baby*, which was another reason why Trace had thought to mention it to the reporter. However, rather than going south towards the Rickenbacker Causeway, Reymond went north.

A duo of neon-lit Lamborghinis passed by, blasting hip-hop while periodically revving their engines. A third raced up behind Trace and honked its horn until Trace got the message: They wanted to race. The rear Lamborghini put on its brights, and Trace had to shield his eyes. The lights were intense enough to show him the side of Reymond's face as he turned to check out the honking, make sure it wasn't directed at him.

Reymond pulled off the interstate, and Trace followed. Reymond made a left onto a dark, downtown street and headed towards the Design District. Less than a mile away, he took a lower ramp and descended into the parking lot of a ramshackle warehouse. Trace came to a stop above the ramp. He watched downwards as Reymond parked next to yet another Lamborghini and a black van. Trace recognized this Lamborghini as being the one he'd seen at Shaw's mansion. Jason Shaw was here.

After Reymond got out of his car, he looked up at Trace and pointed at him, laughing. He waved at Trace. He paused as if expecting Trace to wave back. When he didn't, Reymond turned to go inside the warehouse.

Twenty-Three

The poor air quality inside was oppressive, replete with rust and dust. Shaw walked up and down the row of young girls. He looked them each in the eye. They appeared stick-thin but unsoiled, as promised. Their two delivery men stood to the side, dressed in matching, navy-blue coveralls, like what car mechanics might wear. The mini-bus they had arrived in sat parked near the rear garage gate.

Dara and Lionel also stood together nearby, twin bystanders.

"There's only four girls here," Shaw noted. "There's supposed to be five."

"She'll be along later," said the larger of the deliverymen with a slight Eastern European accent. For some reason, he was the only one who spoke.

"How much later?" Shaw asked. "I need her… yesterday."

"Not sure," the deliverymen sneered. "She suffered

some incidental damage. Had to be hospitalized."

"Who put her in the hospital? You?"

The deliveryman shrugged. "Girls won't listen sometimes."

Shaw went to the Asian girl at the end of the line and shoved his fingers inside her mouth. The girl flinched and took a step back, but he held onto her. He forced her lips aside as he inspected her teeth. He did the same to the next girl, a different Asian, making her tooth inspection extra-long since she was missing an upper tooth. Thankfully, the space was far enough back not to be noticeable. She could be used.

The girl squirmed from the discomfort of having someone pry her mouth open for so long. Shaw shook her hard, then held her still.

Next was the Serbian girl who resisted having his fingers inside her mouth by turning her head away. Shaw got annoyed by this and called for Lionel to come over and hold her. Lionel snatched the girl and pinned her arms behind her back. He pulled her head back by her hair. She yelped and her mouth gaped involuntarily. Shaw could feel the other girls tensing up.

"Don't be nervous," he told them. "Don't be nervous. Routine inspection. This is routine."

"Don't be so rough with them, Shaw," Dara put in, overlapping him. "They're scared to death."

There came a knock at the side door. The deliverymen reached inside their overalls for guns or whatever they intended to defend themselves with. Lionel also reached inside his jacket. An occupational reflex.

Shaw moved his hands down, motioning for everyone to take it easy. "It's just Reymond," he said. "Lionel, go let him in."

Lionel nodded and did as he'd been told.

"You speak English?" Shaw asked the girl with the missing tooth, but she only glared at him. Shaw stepped back and regarded them as a whole. "Do any of you speak English?"

The Serbian girl raised her hand. Shaw stepped up to her. He used his index finger to tuck a strand of her hair behind her ear. "You must be Anja," he said. "Anybody mention my plans for you? You're the special one."

The girl nodded and exhaled, visibly willing herself to remain calm.

Seeing her up close, he noticed she was stunningly gorgeous. She might've had some wear and tear from the trip, but with a tight dress, the right make up, and a new haircut, she could've found professional work with a legit modeling agency. Shaw couldn't believe his fortune.

There was a commotion near the door. Everyone looked to see Reymond and Lionel arguing. From what fragments of their exchange he caught, Shaw understood Reymond didn't want to be searched again. They were business partners now. How long was this level of distrust going to go on?

Reymond held his hands out imploringly. "Yo, Mr. Shaw, really? You're going to search me every single time we get together? What kind of partnership is this?"

"Do you have a gun on you?"

"Never."

"Then why would you object?"

"Because I don't enjoy your boy here touching my ass and my balls. *He* enjoys it. It's humiliating, dude. Hundred percent."

"It'll take two seconds."

"Look at my hand! It's still bandaged. I couldn't hold a gun if I wanted to."

"Christ, just shut up and come over here then."

Reymond walked closer. He looked at the girls and a grin spilled across his face. "What is this?" he asked. "*Hola.*"

Shaw placed an arm around his shoulder, side-hugging him. "Which one do you want? Pick one."

Reymond snickered. "What do you mean?"

Shaw noticed the two deliverymen standing there. "You can both leave. Go away. I paid you. What are you staring at?"

The two men looked at each other. They jogged their way to the minibus at the rear of the warehouse and got in. The taller man started the vehicle and backed out.

Reymond pointed. "I want the white one."

"Any of them but her."

He pointed at one of the Asians on the end. "She's hot. I love Asians."

The girl spit at him and missed the toe of Reymond's boot by centimeters.

Gobsmacked, Reymond threw a puzzled look at Shaw. "She spit at me! Who is this girl? She's not one of your dancers?"

Two long steps and Shaw was in front of the girl. He slapped her across her face, hard enough to topple her. She landed face-down on her elbows.

Reymond ran over and yanked on Shaw's arm. "What are you doing, bro?"

Shaw shoved Reymond off of him. "I can do anything I want to these girls. I own them. You want one or not?"

"What are you? A sex trafficker?" Reymond looked at the girls. His hands went to his head and his breathing turned heavy. "You're a sex trafficker!"

"I'm a businessman, Reymond. Don't tell me you're not cool with this."

"No, I am absolutely *not* cool with this! This is evil, dude. Hundred percent!" He glanced around at Shaw and Dara and Lionel, as if seeing them all for the first time. "I've signed a contract with the devil, huh? That's what I've done. That's what you're trying to show me."

Shaw shook his head, scratched his neck. "Didn't expect an ethics speech from you. If you can't handle this…"

Reymond didn't hear him. He was too busy pacing. "This is sick, bro. I might throw up." He stepped closer to Shaw. "I'm assuming you didn't grow up with a sister, did you?"

Shaw rolled his eyes. "Forget it. We'll just go see the damn nightclub. Lionel can escort these ladies to where they need to go. Get them washed up and fed."

He turned his head and found himself confronted by the Glock G43 Reymond stood pointing into his face. "Why would you do that to other human beings?" he asked.

"Where did you get that?" Shaw asked him.

"Found it in my brother's closet. Huge, right? You're going to let these girls go."

Shaw laughed, a deep-throated guffaw. "That's impossible. You'll have to kill me. Sorry."

"Don't say that. I'll do it, bro. I don't mess around when it comes to shit like this. I'll pull this trigger and I'll blow your head off. All of you. I don't care. I'm fucking stupid."

"Why did you bring a gun?"

"During our last meeting, you sort of jammed one up my nose. Remember? I'm against that happening again."

Reymond's sight darted at a movement over Shaw's shoulder. Shaw knew the movement belonged to Lionel going for his gun. A gun blasted and Shaw ducked. His hands touched his head as it filled with ringing. Lionel clutched his shoulder and went to his knees, grimacing but without making the slightest noise. The slave girls screamed and cowered, a couple of them flattening themselves against the filthy floor.

Shaw made a move for his Glock inside its shoulder holster. A second powerful blast sent the gun flying from his hand and it skidded across the floor. The bullet passed through his arm, shredding muscle, tendons, ligaments, and blood vessels in its path. He felt no immediate pain. Adrenaline did its job, though he knew sheer agony was coming. He had maybe ten minutes.

Shaw took a step towards his gun, but his knee failed to support his leg and he fell. He could feel the blood matting his shirt to his skin, flushing out from a waterfall of ruptured veins. He grew light-headed as his sight left him. Shaw closed his eyes.

Twenty-Four

Trace tiptoed towards the warehouse. He pressed himself against the side door and listened for voices or other signs of activity. He didn't have to wait long. The sound of gunfire jolted him back and he drew his gun. He heard girls screaming, then panicked chattering, then stillness. The nearest window was six feet away, so he crept over. He tried to see in but couldn't. The glass was far too frosted with scratches.

He heard a rumbling towards the rear of the warehouse, as if from a large gate opening. Trace eased in that direction, stepping carefully as to not make noise. He heard more rumbling, this time from a large vehicle starting. Sure enough, a dark passenger wagon came racing around the end of the warehouse. It cut through the parking lot and up the ramp. A minibus had left earlier, but this one was smaller. A trapezoid of sodium-yellow light from a streetlamp flashed over the driver, showing him to be Reymond.

Trace reversed his course towards the warehouse door and kicked the door in, his gun pointed. He yelled, "Police!"

He noticed Shaw and Dara first, standing together. Shaw held his bleeding arm with Dara examining it.

"What are you doing here?" Shaw asked him.

"Reymond shot you?"

"How'd you guess?"

"Is it bad?"

"I think I'll live."

"What happened?"

"We had conflicting opinions about something, and the argument escalated."

Meanwhile, Dara walked to where her brother lay. She bent down and shook him angrily. "Lionel! Wake up. Lionel, hey! Damn you."

"Let me take you to the hospital," Trace told Shaw. "You're losing a lot of blood."

"I would love to, but Reymond stole something from me, and I really, really need it back. As in, right this second. Tonight."

"Okay, but hospital first. Otherwise, you'll bleed out."

"You don't understand. I need it back. What he took. Immediately."

"Won't matter if you're dead."

"Why are you helping me?"

"You're a piece of shit, but I can't let you die. Now let's go."

Shaw's attention was taken away by the sight of Dara checking her brother's pulse. She touched his wrist, then his throat. She turned him onto his back, and his girth caused his arm to swing over with a sickening flop. His white shirt was no longer white. More blood pooled around his body. Dara stood and regarded her dead brother with annoyance.

"I always knew this would happen," she said in a low voice. "I've been preparing to stand here and look down at his gunshot corpse ever since we were little. I always knew it."

Trace heard a tap-tap-tap sound and realized it belonged to fat drops of blood dripping to the floor from Shaw's sleeve.

"'Corpse?'" Shaw asked Dara. "He's dead?"

"My brother is dead," she said.

"Shaw, hospital," Trace reminded him. "I don't know how you're standing up."

When Dara walked back to them, Shaw informed her they were going to the hospital. She agreed and they left the warehouse. Once outside, Shaw wobbled, and Dara caught him. His blood coated her face and hands, now added with her brother's.

"I'm feeling pretty weak," Shaw confessed. "Mind if we take my car?" he asked Trace. "I don't want to get blood all over yours. I'll ruin it."

Trace kept walking toward the Mustang. He was about to lament the Lamborghini's lack of space for the three of them, but a hard blow landed across the base of his skull. He crumbled to the gritty asphalt where he chipped an upper incisor tooth. Gravel stuck to his tongue while he snored soft, inhaling and exhaling the same small spray of dirt.

Twenty-Five

The serial killer sat in his car, not sure of what to do. He opened his glove compartment and removed his .38 revolver, a year-old gift from his father. With the gun tucked inside the waistband of his jeans, covered by his T-shirt, he walked towards where he'd witnessed the detective get knocked out, only a few yards from the warehouse. The detective lay on his stomach with his head turned to the side.

If this detective knew he was being tailed, he'd given no sign of it. The serial killer managed to keep a safe distance the entire way from his house, following in his car. He'd wanted to find out what the detective knew. Get rid of him if necessary. He wasn't thrilled about the idea of murdering another cop, but prolonging his mission took the heaviest weight. Although never unaware he would end up sacrificing his life, the main goal was to take as many people with him as possible.

To his dismay, the detective did not leave to go spy on Jason Shaw as he'd been urged. He drove to South Beach where he double-parked on the street and seemed to wait for someone, then followed that someone himself. This two-way vehicular tail chain proceeded all the way to downtown Miami. When the detective parked his old car atop the ramp, the serial killer pulled over a few yards back, opposite side of the road. Soon, a black minibus sped up the ramp and down the street. He got out. He watched as the detective left his car and eased down the ramp towards the warehouse, then gunfire and another black van speeding away. The detective soon came back out of the warehouse accompanied by a man in a suit, holding his arm, a gunfire victim. A young woman in glasses helped him walk. The detective turned his attention from them for only an instant, but that was all it took. The man took a gun from the young woman's purse and walloped the detective over his head. The pair fled in a Lamborghini, the young woman struggling visibly to navigate this large, luxury car away from the scene. She made it up the ramp and peeled off in the same direction as the other two vehicles.

Was it possible for the serial killer to be so charmed? Providence had struck again. Here was his target laid out and ready for disposal. This was too easy.

He walked back to his car and opened his trunk. Fearful of hidden cameras, he pulled a baseball cap low over his face and walked the ramp down to the warehouse. He returned to the unconscious detective. He nudged him with his foot, and the detective groaned without moving. The serial killer grabbed him beneath his arms and turned him over. He dragged him back up the ramp and towards the rear of his car. It took some effort lifting him over the lip of the trunk, but after a great deal of grappling and shoving, he managed to get him inside. He maneuvered the man's legs around to make room and shut the trunk. He got back into the driver's seat.

He thought of where to take him. He considered shooting him in the head right here and now until he heard sirens. Spooked the sirens might be coming his way, he started his car and rushed off. He went back the way he came. He drove aimlessly for a few minutes, then decided the Everglades would be a good spot for dumping his body. So far away though. This would allow too much time for him to wake up and make this complicated.

The serial killer sat at a downtown traffic light. He ruminated over a better dumping spot, and it came to him like a miracle. He meant to torch the place anyway. It was the perfect location. Poetic even. Burn him alive inside that filthy, noisy immigrant lair which had almost ensnared his father's retirement money. The serial killer started his car, grinning, feeling downright giddy about the idea. His stomach warmed with fire. He felt happy.

Twenty-Six

Shaw's priceless antique couch became drenched in his blood. This happened despite Dara having carefully washed his wound with soap and water. She dried both the entry and exit wounds before applying clean bandages. She inspected his bullet holes for swelling or pus but couldn't find any. The bullet had gone clean through. She went to the kitchen and located a plastic bag, filled it with crushed ice, and returned to him. She pressed the ice onto his arm.

He remained an obedient patient apart from her having to occasionally fuss at him to keep the arm elevated above his heart. After propping his arm on a stack of large pillows, Dara disintegrated into the far end of the couch. She buried her head into her hands and wept. Shaw sat there stunned, not sure of what to say. He'd never seen her emotional before, though she certainly owned reason for it now.

At first, from Shaw's insistence, she'd driven them

around looking for Reymond and the girls, but the pain in his arm became too great and he nearly passed out again. Dara drove them home where she gave Shaw a Percocet and dressed his gunshot wound.

He reached over and touched the small of her back. "I'm sorry about Lionel," he said. "We'll go back and get him." He'd been so desperate to recover his girls that they'd abandoned her brother's body in the warehouse.

"It's all over," Dara whimpered. "Everything is over." She took her hands from her face, showing him the tears striping her cheeks, blending with some of his blood there. "I told you not to go into business with that asshole! But did you listen to me? Do you ever?" Dara sat forward and placed both feet on the floor. She shook her head slow. "You killed my brother."

She launched herself at him and he had to raise his one good arm up to block a round of blows from her. This caused a tremendous amount of pain to his wounded arm, so he was forced to knock her back onto her side of the couch, far more forcefully than he would have ever done otherwise.

"Dara, snap out of it!" he shouted at her. "You're no good to me like this."

She took a moment to recompose herself, then lifted her face. "Call him. Do it now. You have to offer him money or something, *anything* to get those girls back. Offer him whatever he wants."

"He shot me, and he shot your brother. Fuck him. He gets nothing."

"I've reached my breaking point, Shaw. This is too much. I can't anymore."

With some effort, he took his cell out of his blood-soaked jacket, scrolled through the screen, making it sticky with more blood. He landed on Reymond's phone number and pressed it. Reymond answered after only two rings.

"That was a serious fuck-up," Shaw told him. "Where are my girls?"

"They're here with me. They're eating pizza."

"Where are you?"

"Your mother's house."

"Mm-hm, and what are your plans, Reymond? You do recall we have a business contract together."

"I'm not thrilled about this development either."

Shaw drew a deep breath. He felt the newest Percocet dose starting to work. A soothing euphoria seeped through his pores like a pleasant breeze. It ballooned his head until it filled the entire room. "I have a yummy idea," he said. "You bring my girls back to me this instant and I let you live. We'll pretend this never happened. You made an extreme error in judgment. That's all."

"These girls thought they were coming to Miami to work as fashion models. How could you deceive them like that?"

"Go to the police then! Turn them over. I'll deny everything. And who are they going to believe, Reymond? A wealthy pillar of the community who's donated millions? Or some shit-for-brains immigrant with a criminal record?"

Reymond groaned. "I ain't no immigrant."

"You have one hour to bring them back to me, then I'm sending everyone who works for me after you. There won't be anywhere you can hide." Reymond started to respond, but Shaw cut him off. "One hour!"

He ended the call.

Dara wiped fresh tears away. She sniffled. "We have to go get Lionel."

"After we get the girls back."

Shaw got up from the couch and took the stairs to the basement. He went to his rifle cabinet and unlocked it. With his good arm, he removed a bolt-action rifle and, using his torso for leverage, he opened the breech by moving the bolt handle upwards, then back as far as he could pull it. He reached into a drawer and found a magazine. He placed it behind the breech, through the stock and clicked it into place. He slid the round inside until it felt secure. The bolt head extracted a bullet from the magazine, and the rifle was ready to fire. So was Jason Shaw. He took the stairs up out of the basement, prepared to shoot every man in sight if he had to.

Twenty-Seven

Tiny elves used tiny jackhammers to drill into the back of Trace's skull. He tried to sit up, but forces held him back. The unexpected resistance created more pain in his skull, a throbbing that refused to subside. Why couldn't he move?

A full bucket of cold water splashed across his face and the front of his body. The sensation was electrifying, but not in a good way. Trace cried out and his head flung back, jolting his neck. He gritted his teeth and squeezed his eyes shut, which seemed the only form of pain management currently available.

"Sorry," he heard a young male voice say. "I'm tired of waiting. You were taking forever to wake up."

Trace blew excess water from his lips while trying to find adequate oxygen. He coughed and spit. He opened his eyes but couldn't see. He tried to remember how he'd gotten here, and where was here? His vision returned but kept rolling. The wall flipped onto the roof, and the roof flipped onto the floor again. Sparkling dots of light floated around him. He wanted to take his own head off and set it down somewhere.

"Where am I?" Trace asked.

"You don't know this place?" the voice asked him.

Trace tried turning his head, but the pain at the base of his skull was excruciating. He attempted once more to move, but realized his arms were fastened behind him. His legs were stuck to the front legs of the chair. He was tied up.

Once his sight became completely unclouded, he recognized where he was: *Sweet Demon Love Baby*. The nightclub. It was late at night, but there were halogen lamps everywhere. The outline of a person stood nearby. No one else. They were surrounded by renovation debris, including sawdust, stepladders, drop cloths, and such. He recalled how the nightclub itself was an oceanfront complex with an outdoor courtyard area, comprised of cabanas nestled between palm trees.

"Who are you?" Trace asked the outline.

"We met tonight. At my dad's. Forgot me?"

Trace squinted. The person's face came into focus. He did look familiar, but a name wouldn't come. His blonde hair was shaved on the sides with long bangs swept back. He wore the same yellow and orange collared shirt and ripped jeans he'd worn at dinner.

He wasn't sure where the name came from, but it

entered Trace's mouth, and slipped out into the air: "Wally," he said.

"You *do* remember me!"

"Wally, untie me. I don't know how I got here."

"I'm the one who brought you here, dummy. I busted the lock."

Trace let this compute, neurons still scrambled, struggling to rediscover a formation for the world. "Who tied me up?"

"Wow, that guy hit you hard, huh?"

That guy. It was the trigger phrase which brought the entire evening back. Trailing Reymond. Finding Jason Shaw with a gunshot wound. Trying to get him to a hospital. Then—darkness. Blindness and pain. He couldn't piece together what he was doing here in the club though.

"Wally, where's your dad?" he asked.

"At home."

"What-what's going on? You're going to set me on fire?"

"I'll show you." Wally picked up a metal can with a nozzle. He tipped it and began sloshing gasoline over the bar, then randomly onto the floor. He next wetted down the area behind the bar. He dropped fuel over the tables and chairs. The benzene inside the gas stung Trace's nostrils and he gagged.

He struggled against his restraints as a reflex, but there was no give. Not an inch. Kid knew how to tie rope.

"Why are you doing this, Wally?" he asked. "This

doesn't make sense."

"Can you believe my own father was about to invest in this horrible place? He got smart though. He usually does."

"Wally, you need to untie me. Chief Fulcher's not going to be cool with this."

By this point, Wally had upended the gas can and was shaking it to get the last drops out. He made it as far as the pool tables. When the can emptied, he tossed it to the floor where it tumbled. "That was all of it. I was going to dump some over your head. Damn."

"Wally, come on. This is murder."

This brought Wally closer. He towered over Trace and seemed to enjoy this superiority in height. "I killed your spic girlfriend," he said. "I didn't know she was your girlfriend until dinner tonight though. I also killed your spic partner. And I killed another stripper named Camila. Oops."

"Camila is still alive."

"How do you know?"

"Wally, why are you doing this? Your father's the chief of police!"

In response, Wally took a lighter from his front pocket. The terror this brought on Trace made him freeze from the solitary fact that the lighter was light-blue. A calming color. He hoped to own such a lighter someday.

Wally kept on, "A man in your line of work should know more than most that our country is under attack. Foreigners come here uninvited. Refuse to assimilate. Refuse to learn English. They're uneducated. Dad complains about them all the time. I'm only doing what he would do if he could."

Trace closed his eyes. This was worse than he thought. "Wally, my guy, I think you're a little confused."

"I am confused. It's true. See, I was in line for a scholarship, one I'd been aiming for since elementary school. I did the work. I had the grades. That scholarship was mine. Except, nope, it wasn't. The scholarship went to Emilio Simon Ares Cruz because he was a minority, and I wasn't. Yes, I am very confused."

Trace thought carefully on how to respond. He could agree with what he was saying, just to get on his side. He could try reasoning with him. Or he could attempt both. "I get that you're pissed," Trace said, measuring the words, "but is the solution to throw away the rest of your life? You lost a scholarship and now the world must pay? Those people you killed, Wally, what did they have to do with your scholarship?" As he spoke, Trace watched the light-blue lighter bouncing in Wally's hand, never feeling such dread from such a simple device. A single spark and he was toast. Had to keep the kid talking. Buy time.

"You shouldn't have come over for dinner tonight," Wally said. "You should've resigned. What can I say? You're in the way."

"You won't escape from this. I'll be your last victim.

You've crossed the line."

"I imagine at some point I'll be killed, too. And that's okay. I've come to accept it. Any real man should be willing to give his life for something he believes in. Wouldn't you?"

Trace shook his head. He was out of words. He couldn't think of what else to say or do except to start begging for his life. The kid's mind seemed made though. And he was a kid. Just a kid.

"How did you know Nora?" Trace asked, trying to sustain their dialogue. With any luck, the gasoline would dry. "She was the love of my life."

"She gave excellent lap dances. That's for sure. She was the only one who would let me touch her ass sometimes."

"You met her at The Club Cabana?"

"She was my favorite dancer. Definitely."

"When did they start allowing children in?"

"I have a fake ID. And I'm not a child. Don't you dare call me that."

"Prove it. Untie me so we can work this out, Wally. It's never too late."

He flicked the lighter and it produced a small flame. "It is too late though."

"Hey, please, don't, okay? Please! *Please*?" Trace tested his bindings again, forceful enough he nearly fell over.

"I have to do this before the gasoline dries." Wally bent down and lit the gas on the floor. A large swath of flames erupted across the floor so rapidly, Wally had to jump back. He narrowly avoided getting set ablaze himself. The fire spread up the side of the nightclub's walls, then traveled the length of the bar. A set of curtains dissolved from a blanket of orange light as it flowered across the ceiling.

"Place is going up like it's made of straw!" Wally cried out. "Beautiful!"

With a last glance at Trace, he darted out the front door, not bothering to close it. There didn't seem to be time. Wally was right. The club was fully aflame in seconds. The fire had already reached Trace's feet.

Twenty-Eight

Reymond sat in his little brother's wicker chair, which he had come to prefer over any others. The wide back made it feel like a throne of sorts. The four young girls sat on various furniture and surfaces throughout the apartment while finishing the pizza Reymond had ordered. The girls ate ravenously, having not been fed that entire day. He helped dress them in whatever clothing he could find from Enrique's wardrobe. Enrique had been a somewhat petite man, though not puny. Despite their lack of feminine aesthetic, the surfing T-shirts and track shorts fit the girls fine.

Reymond did his best to play it cool with them, like he knew what he was doing. He was fascinated by Anja and felt the need to impress her. She was one of the most beautiful women he had ever laid eyes on, though he felt this way often about the opposite sex. Anja carried a delicate, slender figure, curving inwards from her plump breasts down to her waist before swelling outwards to form her hips, so supple, so dripping-sexy-delicious as to convince any skeptic of a Creator. Her skin was a lucid cream color, which glistened. And her eyes—broad, expressive, almond-shaped mirrors that drank you from beneath pencil-thin brows.

Two of the other girls moved about the apartment. They inspected certain items such as framed pictures and the surfboard hanging over the kitchen entrance. They seemed to think this was the apartment they were meant to arrive at all along. They were attractive as well with cocoa-shaded skin and ink-black, needle-straight hair spilling to their middle backs. Reymond had to remind himself they were minors. Avert his eyes at every chance.

"What is going to happen to us?" Anja asked him, her accent landing sharp over her *t*'s.

"You're going to be all right," he assured her. "I'll probably turn you over to the police. They'll know what to do."

"But they will send us home and we're right back where we started. Probably worse. Those two girls there are Chinese, and they'll be arrested for prostitution as soon as they step off the boat. It won't matter they were forced."

"What about you?"

"I'm in a different situation. I can't go home either."

"Sweetheart, anything is better than what that man had planned for you."

"Are you so sure? What did he say when you called him?"

Reymond noticed the young Malaysian girl on the bed who watched them speaking to each other, not having any idea what was being said. She looked almost young enough to still play with dolls.

"Mr. Shaw demanded I bring all of you back, or he was going to hunt me down and kill me."

"You believe him?"

"I'm deciding."

A siren went by outside and everyone's head turned at the sound. They stayed motionless and grew tense as the siren turned a corner and sped closer. Reymond crept to the window and saw it was a police car screaming down their street towards the apartment. He held his breath as the squad car reached even with the building but kept going. It raced up the street until no longer visible, and the siren faded into silence.

He pivoted back to the girls. "I'm going to figure something out. I can't stand by and let you become sex slaves though."

Anja sighed wearily. "I believe, deep down, we all knew what we were getting into. We signed up anyway. We were desperate."

"I can't allow women to be treated like that. I have a sister, so I know. It's not right."

"You've decided that for us, have you?"

He looked around at them. "Yes, I have."

The pair of Chinese girls had opened the fridge and

were looking through it. One of them came out with a half-jar of orange juice. She opened it and drank directly from the jar. A serene sadness fell over Reymond as he watched this unornamented moment of basic humanity—a young girl drinking, wearing clothes that weren't hers and were never meant to be. The hopelessness of their situation sank in for him.

"What would you do if you were me?" he asked Anja. "Want me to take all of you back to Mr. Shaw?"

Anja balanced her arms out behind her, propping herself up while she sat back. "We have no other hope. No other home to go back to. Anyway, he has our papers."

"So you're going to let strangers fuck you day and night and hope you don't get AIDS? Think about what you're choosing."

"All I care about is my family. If this is how I can best take care of them, I'll do it. I don't care about myself."

"The other girls feel this way, too?"

"I don't know about the Malaysian girl because none of us speak Malaysian, but the others, yes. We can't go back."

Halfway through her speech, Reymond began shaking his head. "I'm not taking you back to him. No way. Hundred percent. I can't do it."

"Maybe you will be the one to care for us?"

"Me? I'm, uh,…" The words clung inside his throat. Being a pimp was not in his skill set. He'd only wanted to go legit and open a business with his brother like they had always talked about. Somehow it had come to this. It was too much. He had to call somebody. He needed help. A lot of help. He knew no one, not here in Miami, not anymore. He was only able to think of one person, and that person might actually have an idea about what to do. Reymond flipped through his phone's contact screen. He had to scroll back up, but he located Trace's number. Reymond clicked the number and brought his phone to his ear. Trace's line rang and rang until a recorded message invited the caller to leave a message. After the beep.

Reymond's message was too large, so he hung up. So be it. He was on his own.

Twenty-Nine

Trace was unaware of his phone ringing because he was almost on fire. Immense flames chewed at the patchwork paneling of his late-partner's beloved establishment. The fire digested it in the form of swelling, black smoke. Trace stomped the flames at his feet as best he could, but the fire kept inching back, bigger and stronger every time. He couldn't keep this up. He had maybe two minutes before the ceiling collapsed. He struggled against his bindings so hard he nearly fell over again. He decided to go ahead and let it happen, see if he couldn't find a better position on the floor. He landed hard onto his shoulder, grunting from the impact. He twisted his shoulders while working his legs and managed to kick his right leg loose. He straightened and bent the leg to work the circulation back. A wooden beam swirling with fire nodules cracked and fell from the ceiling. It crashed a mere three yards away.

Trace thought he heard sirens, and this gave him renewed hope, gave him the strength to keep fighting. He wasn't going to die. Not tonight. Not yet. He couldn't allow himself to become yet another victim to the same psycho who had killed Nora and Enrique and who knew who else. There had to be a way out of this.

However, the more he fought against his bindings, the more he realized how useless his free leg was. Kicking it did little else except spin him around on the floor. Also, the sirens weren't close enough. They wouldn't make it in time. He needed rescue this second. A minute ago. The flames crept closer. He yanked his shoulders around and tried to ignore the pain in his joints, yet there was no give. Too many knots. He would have to be a contortionist capable of dislocating his shoulders, so he could bring them backwards in front of himself. He was capable of no such thing.

The southern wall became completely engulfed in flames and met up with the flames from the ceiling. He heard a sharp cracking noise above and felt the fear pulsing throughout his body. That sound indicated the ceiling was losing integrity and likely on the very verge of falling. He felt his right leg coming looser, but it wasn't enough. He was running out of time. Death was here.

He committed to the final action he could possibly try in saving himself. He yelled for help. He cried at the top of his lungs, straining his throat with only the words "help" and "help me" over and over. Since Wally had left the door open, he could see a small group of people gathering outside. Probably people from the neighborhood who had seen the flames and wandered over to watch the place burn down. He could see a shift in their postures as they caught the sound of his cries. None made a move to help though. They looked at each other, alarmed but confused. What should they do? Should they do anything?

Trace's lungs filled with black smoke, and he felt himself losing consciousness once more. He coughed, then couldn't stop coughing.

From the corner of the leaning doorframe, a person peeked in. They hesitated, assessing the risk. It was a young woman, judging from her frame and height, doing her best to pinpoint the location of whoever was in trouble. She placed her arms over her head and ducked inside. She raced over to him.

"Trace?" the woman asked. It was Janis, the reporter. She attempted to untie him.

"We don't have time for that!" he tried telling her, but his voice was gone, overcome with smoke. Janis peeled at the rope, frantic, making a squeaking noise out of frustration, which was turning into panic. The entire building began to lean. The sound of flames was deafening, and soon she was coughing uncontrollably with him. Thick, pendulous smoke occupied much of the available space inside the club. In less than a minute, they would both be dead of asphyxiation.

Trace licked his lips and pushed his face towards her in a last, feeble attempt to get her to hear him. "Drag me," he managed to say. "Drag me out!"

"Yeah, yeah," she said, as if she'd now realized this was the best idea herself.

Janis moved to get behind him and picked up the back of the chair. He was too heavy. She needed help.

A car-sized chunk of the roof gave way and landed behind Janis. She screamed and dropped him. She stepped away. He slammed his head but couldn't feel anything anymore. He watched Janis momentarily contemplate running outside to save herself, but she didn't. She returned to the back of his chair. "I'm going to get you out of here," she said, though more to herself.

She could only get the chair a few inches off the ground, so she placed her entire strength into dragging rather than lifting. She made it halfway towards the door when a burning stick struck her back. It rolled off her and onto the floor but frightened her enough to drop him again. The frame of the building tilted lower, then lower. The burning roof sunk with it and hung only a couple yards above them. Though she was on her knees, Janis kept pulling at his chair, kept inching him closer to the door. Once she'd reached the doorway, the group of people watching decided it was perhaps time to help. They rushed to Janis and Trace's aid and pulled them both the rest of the way out. With the strength of these additional people, the rescue quickened until everyone was a safe distance from the burning building.

Sirens came closer as the nightclub finished crumbling. The last part left was the dark-chocolate, wooden sign with "*Sweet Demon Love Baby*" etched in magma-red, cursive lettering. The sign melted and read "Demon Love," then only "Love," as even that word distorted into charcoal.

Janis and the bystanders worked together in loosening Trace's rope. There was excited muttering as more people joined the commotion.

Trace went to thank each of them at-length but found that smoke had inflamed his airway. This caused it to swell and partially block his oxygen. He realized he was suffering from acute respiratory distress, which he knew could turn into respiratory failure if untreated. He couldn't guess at how many toxic compounds he'd inhaled, possibly even creating cell damage to his body. Gray mucus oozed from his nostrils from the burnt particles inside his trachea and lungs.

Janis handed him a water bottle and he guzzled from it. He puked the first gulps but returned to drinking without pause.

With the aid of the fresh water and plentiful oxygen, he regained his voice enough to whisper. "Janis, what the hell are you doing here?"

"You told me to meet you here."

"I meant tomorrow morning."

"I thought you said tonight."

"It's fine. Not complaining."

The release of held tension in his shoulders and back from being tied-up was practically orgasmic. He glanced up and saw Janis' fellow rescuers were two men in matching orange-sherbet tank tops and Bermuda shorts, accompanied by a heavyset woman with purple hair. Others might've scolded them for not helping sooner, but their untying of the rope and the sensation this brought to his newly liberated body made him want to become their lifelong pal. Go for drinks. Attend each other's weddings and funerals.

Trace stood, relieved this was still possible. His knees felt shaky, but he could deal. He remained among the living. He placed his arms around Janis in a warm, thank you-hug, the two of them forever bonded by this kinship in a shared near-death experience. He saw Janis was out of breath. She tried not to cry.

"Still want that story?" he asked her.

She spit and her spittle was black. She coughed hard and black dust spilled from her chin.

"Another story apart from this one?"

Before he could answer, two fire trucks arrived. Their sirens flashed and wailed as an ambulance followed.

"Let's leave," he said. Trace took Janis' hand and led her away. Other bystanders stood dumbfounded as he nudged a path through them. "Where you parked?" he asked her. "I need a ride."

(Letter written by Anja Stanković, translated from Serbian.)

It's so crazy how these people don't even know who they're dealing with. Baba, maybe I come across as this super weak girl who can be forced into doing what other people want, but they're so wrong. I will show them what their disrespect gets them.

I know I'm not making sense. A lot has happened since my last letter, Baba. So much. Too much to write.

When everyone was asleep, I snooped around this apartment we're in and I found a safe. None of you may approve of Uncle Semmy, but he did teach me about safes. About how there's a drive cam connected to a spindle, and the far end of that spindle is threaded by a circular something. I forget the name of it, but the spindle rotates with it as a small drive pin catches against the wheels. It's hard to explain but I can open a safe. I found a few thousand dollars and took it. Money is coming, Baba. Finding this safe gave me an idea. A plan.

I should've thought of it earlier, but whatever I have to do to make it happen now is all I care about anymore. Everything's going to be awesome. I got us.

Your Anja

Thirty

Janis drove Trace back to the warehouse to retrieve the Mustang. On the way, she didn't even ask him who had tied him up or why. She was simply too traumatized from the notion of having almost burned to death. Upon reaching the warehouse, they discovered the Mustang was gone. She eased her car over and stopped. Trace got out and walked around to see if perhaps the car had been moved. The Mustang was nowhere. He prayed the damn thing hadn't been stolen—it was downtown Miami after all. Trace kicked a rock and did a brief frustration dance which included a chorus of profanities. With his singed clothing, soot-coated skin, and burnt-crispy hair pockmarked with bald spots, he imagined he must have made quite the raving derelict.

He ran a hand through his hair and some of it broke off between his fingers. Terrific. He checked the surroundings for a "Tow Away" sign and sure enough found one about five yards away, bolted to a light post. Thankfully the towing company's number was printed on the sign. Trace called them to verify they had taken his car, and, yes, of course they had. A gruff man mumbled their address and told Trace to bring proof of insurance and a driver's license.

Janis drove them to a lot near Biscayne Boulevard, filled to capacity with other impounded vehicles. Trace paid an open-shirted man behind a gated window and ten minutes later the Mustang was brought around to him. When leaving, Trace peeled away from the lot, letting the engine telegraph its own annoyance at being caged.

Afterward, Janis followed him to her apartment near Lincoln Road where she parked her car and got into his. Not until US1 did Janis speak up by asking, "Where are we going? What's this story?"

"We're going to my boss' house. The chief. His son just tried to kill me. He's the murderer."

She didn't seem to register what he'd said. "Maybe we should go to the hospital first?" she asked. "I'll bet we both have lung damage. Look at your hair!"

He reached up and felt his hair. It gave off a sulphureous odor. "I have to go warn Chief Fulcher. About his son. It can't wait."

Janis shook her head and tried to snap out of her stupor. She delved into her purse and extracted a notepad and pen. She tested the pen by scratching its point across a random, empty page, but the pen left only inkless indentions. "Dammit," she said and threw the pen out the window.

"You won't forget anything you're about to wit-ness." Trace told her. "Trust me."

"I like taking notes because it helps me feel re-moved. Objective."

"Just stay by my side and you'll get the whole story. Get it right this time though." Trace coughed. A chalky substance filled his mouth, and he had to roll down his window to spit it out. "Tell the truth. I'm going to need it."

They reached Fulcher's home, Trace's second time visiting in an eight-hour span after not having visited his entire career. The house sat dark and tranquil. Four cars were parked in front. If Wally had returned home, he must have gone straight to bed. Which car was his? What would Trace do if Wally answered the door? Jesus, what if Esther answered? She would probably scream when she saw Trace's overdone-cooked appearance.

With Janis following, he went to the front door and knocked. There was no response, so he knocked harder. The door swung open fast, and this caused them to flinch, their nerves frayed.

Fulcher's hair bunched into spiky clusters, matted from his pillow. Even his mustache looked messy. His bruised eye had turned a myriad of colors, from a dull yellow to midnight-blue. Fulcher looked back and forth between them. "What the hell do you want? What happened to you?" he asked. He shielded his eyes from the small wall lamp above his door. He noticed Janis for the first time. "And who are you, honey?"

Janis stepped forward and held her hand out. "I'm Janis Brown. I write for *The Miami Reporter*."

He shook her hand. "Working late?"

"Your son Wally did this to me," Trace told him. "He's the killer we've been hunting. He just tried to kill me by burning me alive in the nightclub."

Fulcher stepped the rest of the way outside and closed the door behind him. "The hell are you talking about?"

"Sir, I know this isn't easy to take in. But I don't know how else to put it: The killer is Wally."

Fulcher's eyes shrank as he gave Trace a thorough overview, examining his scorched hair and clothing. "So you've come to my home in the middle of the night to inform me that my youngest son is some kind of white supremacist murderer?"

"Look at me, sir. I didn't do this to myself. It was Wally."

"I saved him from the fire," Janis said. "Or, I mean, I helped save him." A large moth fluttered around her head, and she ducked from it. She returned to her place.

Fulcher chewed on his bottom lip and nodded. "Want to know what I think? I think you've been drinking again. I think this is all in your head and you've lost your mind. How dare you slander my son!"

"I'm telling you the truth, Chief."

"Get him to a hospital," Fulcher said to Janis, no longer acknowledging Trace. "Take him anywhere. Get him out of my face."

Trace felt undeterred. "Check if Wally's home. Ask him to come out here."

Fulcher's face turned to stone, his voice cold. "Leave my boy alone. That's an order, detective."

"Do Callaway and Paletti already know? Is that why they've been so slow to solve this?"

"Don't go there. You better leave, Trace."

"Why did you ask me if I thought Wally was some kind of white supremacist murderer? I didn't say anything about him being a white supremacist. Where'd you get that?"

Fulcher motioned at Janis. "Miss, you better take him out of here before I seriously hurt this man. Be smart."

"Look at me!" Trace felt himself trembling. "Look at what your son did to me!"

Janis placed a hand on Trace's chest and nudged him away.

Trace conceded to being coaxed back towards his car, but he wasn't done yelling. "I almost died tonight! Your son nearly burned me to death! You need to wake up to what's happening!"

Fulcher stepped off his porch and advanced as Trace and Janis backed up. "No, buddy, *you're* the one who needs to wake up! Get off my lawn before I fire you again."

"Trace, let's go," Janis whispered. The prospect of

violence seemed to be increasing, and she obviously wanted no part of it.

"Go to the nightclub!" Trace called at him. "See for yourself! It's burned to the ground!"

Trace turned and got into his car. He would re-group, attempt to figure out his next move. Did Fulcher already know about his son? Wasn't possible. He couldn't be aware of what his son was doing and keep letting him do it. Not the chief of police.

Trace started the Mustang as Janis got in beside him. He watched Fulcher standing in the center of his yard with his arms crossed, defiant.

As Trace backed out and drove away, he checked his rearview and spotted Fulcher getting into the white pickup truck, the one with tall wheels and a large, square-shaped grill. Was he going to follow them?

When Trace had driven them a couple of traffic lights away, Janis said, "That's a pretty big story you're tossing my way. You have evidence?"

He shook his head. "Not yet. Just his son's confession to me as he dumped gasoline over everything." He looked at her. "What, you don't believe me either?"

"I'm just saying, no matter what, you're going to need evidence." Janis settled into her seat. She raked her fingers through her hair, exhausted. She didn't seem able to stop shaking her head. "This is…this is wow. Think the chief knew about his son?"

"There's no way to be sure."

There came a loud blast as the Mustang's rear windshield blew out in a spray of shattered, tempered glass. Janis screamed and sank in her seat. She tried fitting onto the floor. Trace swerved and fought to keep the car under control. It was late enough at night, so there was no other traffic. Otherwise, he would've crashed into someone. As it was, he nearly took the car onto two wheels.

He fought the Mustang back under control and checked his rearview to see Fulcher behind him. Fulcher tried steering while holding a revolver out his window. He fired again but the bullet went astray. Trace ducked anyway. He reached over to keep Janis down in her seat.

The next shot hit the Mustang. A shock wave reverberated throughout the car, but Trace had no idea where the bullet had hit. He floored the gas and the Mustang's horsepower helped him keep ahead, though Fulcher remained within shooting distance.

"Oh my God," Janis murmured. She peeped her head high enough to see through the rear windshield. "Oh my God, oh my God, oh my God, oh my God, oh my God."

Another gunshot went off but seemed to miss.

Trace noticed a railroad crossing up ahead, coming to life. The red lights blazed from their mast while a rapid bell dinged. The cross bars steadily lowered. Trace estimated they might have time to cross the tracks before the train, barely.

Janis became hysterical. "There's a train! Watch out

for the train!"

"Hold on," he told her. He kept the gas pedal floored.

Another gunshot hit the Mustang's trunk and caused it to unlatch and pop up. It bounced behind them.

The train's headlights became visible, then the locomotive itself. It was a cargo train, pulling a progression of bulky, freight cars, intermodal containers hauling bulk material. Despite their speed, Trace could feel the ground shaking.

"You have to stop!" Janis shouted. She clenched the dashboard. "You're not going to make it!"

"We will," he said, though nowhere near loud enough for her to hear.

The Mustang barreled towards the tracks where the train was now only a few yards from the road. There was a car already stopped there and Trace swerved around it. The driver of the train must have seen the oncoming collision. He honked an airhorn, 110 decibels.

Trace rammed through the crossbar at full speed, the impact far harder than he'd imagined. The wood was thin but the sound of it rupturing from getting run-through by a car was loud and violent. It dented the front of the Mustang, despite its reinforced metal. The collision splintered the windshield in several places and made it hard to see where he was going.

He sped across right as the train passed and missed his rear bumper by inches. He slowed as he glanced behind them. He checked to see if Fulcher had stopped in time and heard the shrill cry of train brakes. The cast iron discs squeezed and pressed as they fought their inertia. A towering ball of fire erupted around the front portion of the train, which shuddered towards a halt. A shower of golden sparks excreted from its wheels.

Chief Fulcher hadn't made it.

Thirty-One

Reymond learned the nightclub had burned down from a news notification on his phone. It was the first thing he saw after waking up. He called Trace again with no answer and felt fairly sure the guy would never answer another call from him for the remainder of his life. Reymond couldn't blame him. He'd been an asshole to the guy. He wouldn't have answered himself either, but he didn't know who else to turn to. He assumed Shaw had torched the nightclub to eliminate any leverage Reymond might've had left. Score some insurance money. This was probably his plan all along. Reymond was in over his head.

Making matters worse, Anja had kept on the entire night with the idea of him becoming their boss. To "take care of them." Demonstrating the full sincerity of her suggestion, she stripped naked in front of him. She gave him an unobstructed view of her fleshy, large breasts, dotted with rich-brown areolas and up-ward-pointing, dark nipples. Her body was hour-glass-shaped, her skin smooth as marble yet peach-fuzzed. The other girls slept, curled together on the only bed.

He wiggled his pants down and she sat on his lap. He felt himself gloved by her.

He blocked out the other girls sleeping, much too young to see this.

Anja grinded his waist and gasped louder as her movements quickened.

"What are you thinking so hard about?" Anja asked him. She sat on the bed with the other girls, fully-clothed in real life. "You can't take us to the police."

Reymond snapped back to reality. He noticed the girls staring at him while he'd daydreamed making love to Anja. Reymond heard a faraway beeping noise. His phone. He fingered it free from his front pocket and saw it was Trace calling him back.

"I need your help," Reymond told him. He looked over his shoulder at the girls. One of them had fallen back asleep. The other two played with their phones.

"What kind of help?" Trace asked.

"I found out Shaw is a sex trafficker. He's a super, duper, ultra-extra, wicked man."

"I seem to remember telling you that. And *now* you want me to help you do something about him?"

"You have to help me, dude. Do it for Enrique."

"What have you done?"

"Something *mucho loco*. I kidnapped some of his

girls. I was trying to do the right thing."

"Kidnapped?" He could hear Trace trying to piece this together in his mind. "From the warehouse? This is why you shot Jason Shaw?"

"Yeah, the warehouse. I saw you tailed me."

"Where are the girls?"

"I'm looking at them. Please, I don't know what to do. They want me to take over their ownership."

"That's bonkers. Take them to the police and turn them over. What's wrong with you?"

"Thing is, my record? My reputation? They'll arrest me immediately. *You* need to do it."

"I've got too many things going on, Reymond. I can't get involved in this now."

"Mr. Shaw said I have one hour to bring them back or he's going to hunt me down and murder me."

"Then you better give them back."

"Time out, time out. Let's help each other."

"Last time I tried that you didn't just stab me in the back, you cut my head off."

"I was a dick. I admit it. I'll never do it again."

"I don't trust you. I can't afford to. Go take care of this on your own."

"Do it for Enrique," Reymond lowered his voice, doing his best to sound wounded. "He was my brother. You can't let Enrique's *brother* get killed, too."

"I'm not turning those girls in. I don't work vice. I'll find you a phone number."

"If you won't turn them in for me, at least go with

me when I give them back?"

"There is absolutely no way in Hell."

"Trace, he's going to kill me! Come on, dude. He burned down the club last night! He's insane!"

"That wasn't Shaw."

"How do you know?"

"Never mind that. I can give you a number."

"I can't call the cops! I won't. These girls are freaked out about getting deported. Mr. Shaw has their papers."

"If I went with you over to Shaw's, that would make me an accomplice to sex trafficking, Reymond, and the answer is no."

"You're not an accomplice to shit! Just have my back. For ten minutes. Fifteen tops. Nothing will happen."

Trace kept objecting, declaring continuously that he didn't trust him. An argument erupted in which Reymond begged him to please, please, please give him another chance. He'd learned his lesson. His life was on the line here. Reymond managed to wear Trace down.

"We're only going to drop the girls off and leave," Reymond assured him for the hundredth time. "That's it. We're gone."

"Where are you?" Trace asked.

"My brother's."

"Goddammit, you're lucky you're Enrique's family. We'll be right there."

"We?"

Trace had hung up.

Though the Asian girls turned out to know more English than they'd first let on, he still spoke only to Anja since she understood English the best. He told her, "I'm taking you back to the man who paid for you." He held his hands out, pleading with them. "I have no choice. I'm sorry. I can't become some half-ass pimp for you. And I can't take you to the cops because I have a record. I made a mistake. A big mistake."

Anja stood as though she meant to strike him. She crossed her arms.

"Hey," he cut her off, "you can walk out that door anytime you want. Be free. All of you. Welcome to America."

"And go where? We're illegal and we have no money. We have absolutely nothing."

"At least Shaw can afford to buy you clothes. I can't. And I'm in enough trouble anyway. I'm sorry."

Anja rolled her eyes. She dropped her arms.

"Okay," she said. She punched his chest. "Take us back."

Thirty-Two

Trace drove Janis back to his apartment where both of them fell asleep in minutes, Trace on the futon and her on his papasan lounge chair. After showering, he cleaned his Glock. He replaced it inside a shoulder holster, which he wore under a thin, blue blazer. He took Janis to breakfast before meeting up with Reymond.

The poor young girls eyed these new people suspiciously, uniformly glowering. They seemed less than pleased with America so far. Trace knew they were also likely displeased with being returned to Shaw. Reymond, for his part, seemed uncharacteristically quiet and sullen.

Trace followed Reymond's SUV. Partway there, Trace looked at Janis, checking on her, but she was staring out her window, watching the scenery swipe by. It was the scenery of a world forever changed for her probably. She was learning she couldn't just write about the world burning without getting scorched herself. Literally.

He considered calling the FBI. They might be interested in this exchange they were having. Chances were, the FBI had at least some clue what Jason Shaw was up to. No way someone so high profile could keep such a secret. Trace went to grab his phone, but Janis made a whimpering sound.

"You all right?" he asked her. He touched her arm.

"If you don't mind, I believe I would rather go back home," she said. "This is more than I can cope with."

"This isn't normal for me either. It's the least normal week of my life."

"I want to go home though. Can you take me home? I need to go home." She held her hand on her door as if she meant to drop out while the car was moving.

"I'll take you home," he told her, but staring straight ahead. "After you witness and document one last event for me. I promise."

She shook her head.

"What?" he asked her.

She kept shaking her head. "I want to go home."

—

The two vehicles arrived at Shaw's mansion, Reymond with the lead, getting them buzzed in. Again Dara answered and opened the gate for them. After he parked the SUV, Reymond opened the back door and the girls stepped out on the same side, one after the other, blinking and yawning, hands inside their shorts. Trace walked behind the girls with Janis shadowing him, bringing up the rear.

Surprisingly it was Shaw who opened the front door, his dressed arm in a sling as he watched the seven of them walking up. His eyes fell on Trace and Shaw recoiled. "What the hell happened to you?"

"It's been a rough week," was all Trace could think to say.

"Sorry I shot you," Reymond said to Shaw, as if apologizing for something offensive he might've said. A month ago. He offered his hand to shake.

Shaw glanced at the extended hand with its unwrapping, bloody bandages. "Give me my girls back and go die somewhere," he told Reymond.

"Can we come in and talk first?"

Shaw laughed and looked around at everyone. "About what?"

"About us. Our partnership. Where do we go from here? Why did you go and burn down the club?"

"The nightclub burned down?"

"You're a good actor."

Shaw furrowed his brow, his face turning red. "I don't have time for your games. I should kill you right where you stand. Shooting me? I can take a bullet. But you killed my head of security who was also my personal assistant's brother, you fucktard."

"Hey, hey," Trace interjected. He stepped between them and spoke to Reymond, "We did what we came here to do. Now let's leave as we agreed."

"No, I'm not going anywhere," Reymond said. "I'm not done."

"What are you talking about? You *promised*."

"I'm not leaving here until I have some conditions met."

Trace went to clutch his head in grief and anger but brought his arms back down. He considered punching himself in the face for being so gullible. When would he learn? He thought back to that phrase in Nora's diary: *Maybe any second. Maybe never.* Didn't matter anymore though. The drain plug had been pulled.

Shaw looked at his girls and curled his finger at them, motioning for them to come inside. He stepped back from the door so they could file in, which was what they did. "Where did they get these hideous clothes?" he asked no one in particular.

"They were my brother's," Reymond said as he walked by Shaw and inside his home.

Trace followed with Janis and, once within, they were both thrown against the wall by large men in suits. They were patted down and molested for weapons.

"Looky here," one of the guards said. He held up Reymond's gun which he'd discovered inside his jacket.

The guard searching Trace found his Glock inside his jacket as well. "I got one, too," he said. He held the Glock with two fingers upside-down.

Shaw looked at them with his head tilted. "You're kidding me."

"I forgot I had it," Reymond said. "Relax. You can keep it. Hundred percent."

"I'm police," Trace said. "I always have a piece on me. I would like it back now."

"You're not police," said Shaw. "Think I forgot?"

He motioned for the guard to give him Trace's gun. He took the gun and pointed it at Reymond. "Any last words?"

"We have a contract!"

"You just told me the nightclub burned down. Why do I need you anymore?"

Reymond was about to respond when Shaw leaned his head back and bellowed: "Hey, Dara!"

She appeared atop the second level. She saw Reymond and her jaw tightened. Trace caught this and knew they absolutely had to split from here somehow. Soon as humanly possible.

"Take these girls upstairs with you," he called to her. "Get them showered and show them to their rooms."

"They're going to live here with you?" Reymond asked.

"For a few days maybe. We have apartments for them elsewhere."

"They're showered. I was able to do that much for them at least."

"Was the nightclub insured?"

"Of course. That's why I figured you burned it

down. Revenge for me shooting you, and for the insurance money."

"I'm normally not so passive-aggressive as that. Dara, take these girls and get them changed. I don't want them to have to see this."

A volley of machine gun fire exploded from upstairs. Everyone covered their ears and cowered. Trace could see dirt kicking up in the front yard from hundreds of bullets. A security guard showed up where Dara had been standing. She had either ducked for cover or retreated somewhere.

"Hey, boss!" the security guard called. His voice quivered with nervousness. "We got a problem."

Shaw started to inquire as to the nature of this problem, but he didn't have to. Numerous cars came pulling up to the front gate. The windows were intermittently painted blue from their siren lights. Men in windbreakers began to fan out and take cover as bullets pinged around them. The gunfire upstairs was joined by more gunfire and the air over the yard became lit up by crisscrossing tracer bullets.

"Get away from the windows!" Trace yelled at Janis and the girls, but everyone was already dashing for cover, fleeing deeper within the house. Trace guided Janis by her elbow as they ran to the sunken living room. It was bordered by thick, concrete walls.

As the gunshots intensified and the front windows of the house shattered from return fire, the girls collectively screamed. Reymond hid there with them, everyone sheltering behind the large, sectional couch. They were only there a minute when Trace spotted the FBI SWAT agents running along the outer gate. They surrounded the place while setting up a perimeter. They wore Kevlar helmets with goggles and military-issue, bulletproof vests. They toted MP5 submachine guns, which Trace knew carried thirty round magazines. Shaw was doomed.

An amplified voice could be heard through a police bullhorn, though Trace couldn't make out what the voice said. He could guess it demanded Shaw give himself up peacefully, though this was obviously too late. As if to answer the bullhorn, there came a fresh round of machine gun fire from upstairs. The FBI agents and police ducked behind whatever barrier they could—a bush, an outer wall section, the door of a squad car, anything.

Shaw stood with his back flat beside a window. He peeked through the outer side of the curtains. Trace noticed that he held a bolt-action rifle now. He looked startled and afraid, then furious. He stomped over to his visitors and sex slaves and stood before them, in full aim of the windows.

"You brought the FBI?" he barked at them. He shouted to be heard over the roar of automatic weapons upstairs.

"Wasn't me, dude!" Reymond answered. He sounded offended. "Why would I trap myself?"

Before Shaw could speak again, the same security guard from earlier reappeared at the inside balcony. "Boss, they got us surrounded. What do you want us to do?"

"Kill them!" Shaw yelled. "Keep shooting! Kill them all!"

More windows disintegrated as bullets pierced the glass into pieces and burrowed into the walls, into different housing appliances. Bullets busted the glass of Shaw's saltwater aquarium and the water gushed out. A colorful multitude of fish flipped and twitched on the floor, their tiny mouths opening and closing, opening and closing, suffocating on air.

At first, Trace assumed the girls screamed from the terror of taking sustained fire. He turned to see they were reacting to one of the Chinese girls lying on her back, a neat bullet hole in the center of her forehead. The hole leaked a thread of blood which rounded both nostrils. Her eyes remained open but empty.

He looked at Janis to find her wobbling, on the verge of fainting. Her lids fluttered. After another round of gunfire shredded the walls of his home, Shaw sought cover behind an overturned, marble table.

Reymond crawled on his stomach to reach Shaw, having to brush aside the glass and dying fish in his path. Meanwhile, objects detonated around him as bullets struck them at a thousand feet per second. The entirety of Shaw's living room was alive with flying or floating debris. A cloud of feathers drifted throughout the mansion, violently expelled from a down cushion somewhere. The noise of glass breaking and sheet-wall getting pulverized was endless, much of it falling loose after clinging to its frame.

"Give me my gun back!" Reymond yelled to Shaw, though they were right next to each other. "I want to help!"

Dara came sneaking down the stairs, a small gun drawn. Bullets hit the stair railing and created a mass spray of splinters. She yiped and fell. She slid the rest of the way down the stairs and rolled, commando-style, until reaching the floor. She crawled on her stomach towards Shaw and Reymond while a rapid round of bullets ripped apart the stairs where she had just been seconds ago.

The Serbian girl got to her feet and ran up the same stairs, leaping over places where steps were missing. Trace watched in wonder as she disappeared within the second floor. She'd made a big gamble that their assailants outside wouldn't fire in the same place twice, evidently opting for the safety of a higher vantage point.

More machine gun fire erupted from up there. This caused a reaction of automatic weaponry to be detonated from every direction. It was deafening.

In sheer panic, one of the other girls ran upstairs to be with the Serbian girl. She only made a dozen steps when her torso became perforated by a series of bullets. The holes in her were so big, Trace could see through her. She fell dead at the foot of the stairs.

Dara crawled to the marble table, which sheltered Shaw and Reymond.

"Hey," Reymond told her, "I'm sorry about your

brother. I didn't know he was your brother."

Dara glared at him until a bullet nicked the edge of the table, removing a triangular-shaped piece, which bounced off her head. She was unhurt though and gave her attention back to Reymond.

"I was just surprised," Reymond continued. He spoke in a conversational tone, as though sitting in a coffee shop surrounded by intellectuals rather than a hurricane of bullets. "I have a problem thinking things through and it gets me in trouble. I'm not a bad person though. Not as bad as you might think."

Dara raised her gun and shot Reymond point-blank in the forehead. He looked at her questioningly as blood spewed down his face. He slumped onto his side. He writhed a moment, seeming like he might try to get up. He went still and didn't move again.

Shaw looked at the dead man next to him, then at Dara. He nodded at her and ducked as a vase exploded behind him. Tiny, ceramic shards sprinkled his hair.

There was a pause in the firing upstairs, as they were likely reloading. One of the rear, sliding glass windows caved in as they took fire from the backyard pool area. Trace saw more agents spilling over a back fence. Two of them found their feet and forged ahead towards the house. They made it half-way, letting their rifles lead the charge as they micro-stepped closer. They reached a spot between both swimming pools where both men jerked backwards from taking bullets to their chests, their uniforms dotted by puckered holes. They fell to their knees. One of them sunk to the ground. The other wiggled a few feet further before another two bullets entered his back. *Holy shit*, Trace thought. All Hell was going to break loose now. What had happened so far was only a warm-up compared to the retaliation coming. Shaw's abundance of outlaw security was going to be his undoing.

The bullhorn sounded again and implored Shaw once more to surrender. Trace couldn't see much but he understood the bullhorn likely belonged to whichever SWAT vehicle served as their mobile command headquarters. It was their procedure to get negotiators in contact with the suspect, gather as much info as possible. Recon units could've been casing his mansion for weeks, and nobody would've had any idea. These guys were stealth experts. It was entirely possible they had drilled a small hole in a wall somewhere and were using a pinhole camera to watch them.

Trace lowered himself onto the floor where the remaining girls had sought shelter. He had to pull Janis down with him from sitting there comatose while bullets sang and zipped over her head. A bullet buzzed his right ear. The living room was filled with bullets, either buried into fabric, wood, or drywall, or rolling on the tiles. He felt absolutely stunned the FBI would unleash such deadly force upon a building without fully knowing who was inside. They only knew they'd been fired upon and *here you go, have some bullets yourself, asshole.*

If current events progressed in this way, everyone was going to die. It was up to Trace to become the peacekeeper, a mediator between warring factions. He decided he would first negotiate with the nearest combatants which were Shaw and his assistant. Trace started to crawl over to them, but another fresh burst of machine gun fire from upstairs was met with a re-sounding answer. He held still, terrified, the adrenaline momentarily rooting him where he was.

Taking a deep breath, he resumed snaking across the floor until reaching the overturned table. He crouched there with them. Reymond lay on his back, a dark-red puddle growing around his head. He stared at the ceiling, his expression still confounded at getting shot.

"Shaw, you need to surrender," Trace told him. "Otherwise, everyone is going to get killed. Every-one. There's no way out of this."

Trace might have expected him to argue, but he merely nodded. Him and Dara scooted themselves closer as more gunfire continued its deluge through-out the house, making mealy holes within holes eve-rywhere. The floor was junked with busted ceramic, glass, fish, and other unidentifiable debris. The ex-quisitely manicured décor lay destroyed.

"I assume you're on their side?" Shaw asked him. He fired his rifle over the edge of the table and ducked down again.

"I just want to live!" Trace shouted to be heard

above the blasting gunfire. "They're firing at me, too!"

"You're not the one who brought them here?"

"Hell no! Do they seem like they're aware of me?"

"I think you know who brought them here," Dara said to Shaw. "It's Charles' people. The ones you never paid. *They* did this."

"Whoever it is, you have to surrender," Trace added. "You're going to get us all killed!"

"I don't care."

"What about everybody else? Your staff? These girls? Think it's fair you get to choose their fate, too?" The gunfire ceased, which found Trace unnecessarily shouting: "their fate, too!"

"What about her?" While speaking to Shaw, Trace held his hand towards Dara. "You don't care about her?"

Shaw seemed to mull over Trace's words. He checked behind him at the one remaining girl cowering in the living room. She sobbed and pressed against the floor, her hands over her head. He looked up, as if trying to see through the ceiling at his men up there. No question they would run out of bullets. They were trapped.

"You have no idea what I've been through tonight," Trace said. His ears rung, so he spoke without hearing himself. "I was almost burned alive tonight. This kid who did it, he kind of reminded me of you, Shaw. Lashing out. Full of hate. So resentful for how he's been treated by the world. This isn't the way to handle it though. Having people die for you? It just isn't."

"I'm not full of hate."

"Look around you. This is coming from a place of love?"

Shaw looked at Dara. Her hair sparkled with crumbs of glass. The hollow notch above her collarbone was spattered with Reymond's blood from when she'd shot him.

"Yes," Shaw told Trace. "It is."

"I see a soul there inside your eyes, Mr. Shaw. It's the exact same as I saw in that boy tonight. Lost. Angry. Hopeless. Doing what he thinks is right, but he's got it all backwards. Now people are dead, and they didn't deserve this. They have families who are going to be getting some horrible news today…"

"Okay, okay, shut up," Shaw said. "If you want to run your mouth so much, go out there and talk to them. Tell the FBI to stop shooting us."

"I need to give them more than that, Shaw."

"Tell them to stop shooting and I'll let everyone out." Shaw shouted at the ceiling: "Hold your fire! Hold your fire! Anybody alive up there?" There was a pause. A voice confirmed everyone upstairs was alive. Shaw turned back to Trace. "Do your thing."

"I will. I'll do my best. This is what's right."

"That and I'm out of ammo." With that, Shaw dropped his rifle. He kicked it aside and winced from a pain in his wounded arm.

Trace rose gently to his feet with his hands up, his

badge displayed in his left hand. He tiptoed towards the front door, which stood opened from the force of so many bullets pounding it. He made it outside, hands still raised. When his eyes adjusted, he was amazed at the sheer mass of force on display around Shaw's property. There was a sea of flashing police lights. He couldn't see the end of them.

"Don't shoot!" he yelled. "I'm a police officer. Homicide Detective Tracey Strickland! The inhabitants have agreed to surrender!"

However, his mangey appearance threw them off. The voice blared from the bullhorn: "Stay exactly how you are! Hands up! Move and we will not hesitate to Swiss Cheese your ass!"

Trace held immobile while a SWAT agent used a Hallagan Tool, a firefighter tool similar to a crowbar, to pry open the front fence. Machine gun pointed, he marched up on Trace. A second agent followed. Once the first agent reached Trace, he planted a foot behind Trace's leg and karate tossed him onto the grass. Trace didn't resist as he hit the ground like a ragdoll, landing on his side. The agent flattened him and pinned him with a knee atop his chest. The second agent snatched Trace's wallet away and inspected his badge. He held it up and waved it at whoever was in charge of the raid.

"Badge looks legit! He's the cop!" Him and the second agent tugged Trace to his feet and hustled him towards the open gate. Once he was among the other FBI agents, the one holding his elbow asked him,

"Nobody told us you were in there. What the hell were you doing?"

"My fucking job," Trace told him.

Thirty-Three

The young, Malaysian girl left the mansion next, walking slow at first, then dashing for the safety of the amassed FBI agents once she got closer. Janis came next, tiptoeing. Next came the remaining members of Shaw's security staff, all five of them. Weaponless, hands behind their heads. Shaw made a mental note to remember this in case he ever felt bad about himself. This made eight lives he'd saved today. Well, with some convincing from Trace.

Still crouched behind the table with Dara, Shaw watched through the busted windows as his men were ordered to kneel. A gang of SWAT agents surrounded them and shoved them to the ground with such force and disrespect that Shaw nearly regretted telling them to surrender. Afterward, his security staff became dragged to their feet and pushed outside the property. He was surprised to see one of them covered head-to-toe in blood, though he didn't seem wounded.

Shaw spotted a familiar figure hovering around Trace, asking him questions. He noticed the man's face was bruised and almost dismissed him as an injured agent, except his bruises weren't fresh. Then it hit Shaw—The man was Douglas, the fat guy he'd nearly beaten to death with his brass knuckles a week ago. The guy was FBI? Who else was?

Shaw observed as a commotion started between Trace and the agents. There was some confusion until Trace took the bullhorn.

"Shaw, we have a girl missing!" he called. "The white girl! She ran upstairs but she didn't ever come out."

"Maybe she's dead?" Shaw waited, unsure if he had been heard or not. "I have no idea!"

"Okay then!" Trace on the bullhorn again: "Your turn, Shaw. Come on out. You and Dara. Put your hands in the air and come out real slow. No guns!"

Shaw looked at Dara who was shaking her head.

"What?" he asked her, genuinely surprised.

"Do you remember that first time you found Lionel and me. When we were little. We were so scared and so hungry. And so…pitiful. But you took us in anyway?"

"And?"

"Shaw, we're going to prison for the rest of our lives."

"Maybe not. I know people."

"I can't stand the thought of not being with you."

"I'm buddies with the mayor. He could get me out of this. Probably."

"Did you hear what I just said?"

"You're perplexing me, Dara."

"I love you, dummy. I love you! God help me, but it's why I've kept working for you. To change you into a better man without being your mother."

He rolled his eyes, truly marveling at this. "You are one crazy bitch, huh?" he asked her, but not without tenderness.

"You didn't know?" She touched the side of his face as well. "No, you knew."

Shaw leaned in and he kissed her. He started to pull away, but she took his chin and guided him back. She resumed the kiss. A small object slid out of his inside pocket and thudded onto the floor. He broke the kiss to see what it was—his brass knuckles, shiny, pretty, and utterly useless in a gunfight. He couldn't help but laugh.

"You should've picked someone better," he told her. "I've lost everything. And here I am surrounded by a thousand cops and FBI agents, all of them praying I come out shooting."

"I say we give them what they want."

"I don't think so."

"I spent half my life in an orphanage. I'm done with being caged."

"I could testify I forced you into everything."

"No amount of money or influence is going to get us out of this, Shaw. Not this."

"You underestimate me."

She grimaced, shook her head. "That cop was right," she said. "You've got things backwards."

Dara got to her feet. She ran forward and out of the mansion. Once outside, she fired her gun back and forth indiscriminately. She made it only a few yards before her torso became ripped by high-caliber fire and she fell. Shaw yelled out and chased after her, by and by feeling what must have been love as he raced into the arms of death. He didn't make it as far as her since he took on more fire. Shaw fell dead and bleeding, his nose buried into the earth, his right hand reaching out.

(Letter written by Anja Stanković, translated from Serbian.)

Baba, you wouldn't believe it. I got trapped in a shootout! I saw people die! Made me completely understand why the war was so haunting for all of you. It's indescribable. I never imagined guns were so loud, especially when there are so many of them! My ears are still ringing.

I saw a girl get shot between the eyes though, and I'd had enough. I couldn't just lie there anymore and wait for my turn. I still had my plan.

I made it upstairs and found the safe in a walk-in closet, where they always are. Uncle Semmy was right—every crook hides money in a safe to keep the government out of it. This Shaw man had security up there, but they were way too busy with shooting. One of them saw me go into the closet but he turned back around. Probably figured I was diving for cover into the most protected place possible. Or he just didn't give a single, living shit right that second.

The safe took five minutes. There wasn't as much cash as I'd hoped, but enough to fill a laundry bag. I left the closet unnoticed and found the attic and hid there until the middle of the next night. The laundry bag never left my hand, Baba. That entire time. I've made the solution to the rest of my life in America. My bag of vouchers to the Promised Land.

I came across some clothes which were probably meant for me anyway and I changed into them. I found a duffel bag for the cash and I left. Just like that. Zblogom!

I know I said I would send you money, Baba, but I can't anymore. At first, I wasn't going to tell you, but I found out from the ship crew it was you and Momma and Uncle Semmy who helped them trick me. They showed me your signature and had audiotape and everything. You sold me into sexual slavery, Baba. You did. All of you. For your own profit. I was going to send you money anyway because that's just how much I love you. A part of me even understands.

Another part of me has been gutted like a fish right down to the core of my soul. I'm a changed person. I won't be sending any of you anything. Not a single thing.

Thank you for this lesson, Baba. I will never forget it.

Thirty-Four

Trace drove back to South Beach with Janis beside him. They had given their stories to the FBI deputy director on-site and were instructed to go straight to the station. Give a rundown on what had happened to them for Callaway and Paletti. Also, there was a major crisis to contend with. Chief Fulcher had died in a drunk driving accident last night. Had driven into a train like it wasn't noticeable.

Trace drove down the causeway, the port of Miami on their right, ice-blue water holding the impossible girth of gleaming, white cruise ships. Towering cranes loaded truck-sized containers onto cargo ships, ready to take them to faraway lands. The sky was cloudless and blue as life.

"Remind me where you live," Trace told her. The engine made a steady ticking sound. Last night's impact with the railroad crossing bar had assuredly done some damage to the Mustang, much of it unseen. He wasn't sure how many more miles it would give him before needing a mechanic. "I'll drop you off."

"But I thought I had to go with you to the police station."

"Go write your story. Make sure I'm the hero. I'll cover for you."

"Won't I get in trouble?"

"Only if you show up with me. You should let me take you home."

"I don't understand. You didn't do anything wrong."

"There was another car at the train crossing last night. A witness. Also there's going to be surveillance tape of Fulcher chasing me and this car is pretty damn easy to recognize."

"I was there though! I can attest for you. Isn't that why you brought me along?"

"Chances are these guys are waiting for me with handcuffs by now. You don't want to be there. I've put you through enough."

She touched his arm. "I can take it, Trace. I'm not a flower."

He stared at her, observing that she was indeed not a flower.

"Everything's going to be okay," Janis added. "I can do it."

Trace came to the first traffic light on South Beach's Fifth Avenue. He stopped and the ticking sound inside the engine went away. He looked at her. "You sure?"

"I told you," she said. "I'm not that kind of reporter."

"I have to stop and see someone first though. At
Mount Sinai. I'll be a second."

"I'll wait in the car for this one."

"Thanks."

The light changed green.

One Week Later...

Thirty-Five

Wally took the baggie of cocaine from his pocket and held it up for Starr to see.

"Fantastic!" she shouted.

They sat in his car inside South Pointe Park, which was empty except for a lone, late-night jogger. He was a dot in the dark distance. Wally had parked by the pyramid-roofed watchtower overlooking the boardwalk, which stretched off into the black ocean, as if bridging the afterworld with this one.

He handed her the baggie, and she held it up to the moonlight. "That's a lot!"

"Yeah, it was expensive," the serial killer said. "I hope it's good."

Starr opened his glove compartment without asking. She leaned forward to peek inside. "We need something to put it on, so we can cut some lines."

Wally looked at the back of her neck, at how skinny it was. She began rummaging through his glove compartment, cramming her disrespect for him right into his face. It was more than he could take. He grabbed the back of her neck and squeezed.

"*Ouch!* What are you doing?" she cried.

He closed his fingers harder until they ached. He needed her jugular to stop her from breathing, but he couldn't reach it from this angle.

"You're hurting me! Quit it!" She sat up and threw her full weight into it. He wasn't sitting close enough to prevent this, so he let go. He reached under his seat for his knife. He found its handle but hesitated.

"You are so gorgeous," he said to her.

Starr sat with her back pressed against her door, her eyes wide, bottom lip shaking. She sat stuck between screaming for help or sobbing with panic. She'd dropped the baggie.

"You were right," he told her. "I killed Nora. I killed that cop. I almost killed Camila. I certainly tried anyway. Now it's your turn. That sucks, no? You scared?"

"What did I ever do to you?" she asked him. He could see she was trying to discreetly find the door handle at her elbow. He grabbed her knee and startled her. She balled her hands in front of her face and squashed her eyes closed.

"You didn't do anything," he explained to her, "except be in the wrong place at the wrong time. It's nothing personal."

"Then let me go!"

"I would but you're not one of us."

"What do you mean? One of who? I'm a human being!"

He shook his head. "You're a foreigner."

Starr bunched her brows together and searched his eyes, trying to find some weakness in there. A chance for mercy. "Please, let me go," she whispered. She started sobbing.

He patted her knee. "There's nothing to be afraid of, okay? You'll go to Heaven. You're better off there anyway."

"Please, don't kill me. *Please...*"

Wally took the knife out, made sure she saw it. "This is in memory of my Father. For everything he stood for!"

There was a knock on the car window behind his head. He turned to see a Glock G24 aimed into his face, the barrel millimeters from the glass.

"Put the knife down, Wally," Trace told him. "Slow. Real slow."

"Surprise, dickhead!" Starr shouted. She brought her legs up and kicked her heels into Wally's stomach repeatedly. He opened his door to escape her. Trace had to stand back but kept his gun pointed.

Wally spilled onto the ground, right at Trace's feet. Wally enclosed his arms around his head. "Kill me," he whimpered. "Get it over with. Just kill me."

Trace kicked Wally's hand until it dropped the knife. Trace grabbed Wally's arm and yanked him to his feet. "Get up," Trace snapped at him. "You're the white American son of a recently deceased police chief. Nobody's going to kill you for this."

Starr came out of the car on the driver's side. Before Trace could stop her, she charged Wally and struck him over his head and body with one of her heels. He held his arms up in an attempt to block her assault. He stumbled in the process and returned to the ground. Starr placed herself over him, taking advantage of her tactical position to better land more blows.

Starr was livid: "You don't want us immigrants here until you need us here and then we're a dime a dozen! Fuck you!"

Trace took a step forward to stop her from seriously injuring the kid. He recalled Fulcher's words to him that night at the dinner table. You're too soft. Too nice. I like my detectives to be tougher. Stop being a pussy.

He took a step back and watched as Starr continued to pummel the serial killer. Perhaps a fate worse than death. Trace lowered his weapon and exhaled. He allowed the serenity to embrace him.

Another Week Later...

Epilogue

Trace entered Camila's hospital room to discover she'd been moved yet again. Where he'd expected to see her healing in peace, most likely asleep, he was instead faced with empty, white, fitted sheets, the bed reclined flat as a standard mattress. He'd learned Reymond was on the same floor, so he decided to go ahead and visit him first.

The positioning combined with the small caliber of Dara's firearm, although fired at close range, had impaired its lethality, resulting in a bullet trajectory which skidded off Reymond's outer cranial structures. In other words, his hard head saved him.

Trace found him sitting up in bed, crowned in gauze, his hand now carrying a small adhesive across its knuckles. Reymond watched cartoons on a wall-mounted television where giant robots and dinosaurs engaged in ferocious battle, much to the detriment of surrounding skyscrapers. Reymond smiled when he saw Trace enter. He motioned him over for a hug, which Trace obliged him with.

"How do you feel?" Trace asked. He tried to break the embrace, but Reymond held on for a couple seconds longer. He let go and Trace stood straight.

"Don't remember a thing," Reymond said. "Well, except the FBI shooting the place all to Hell. Whatever happened to the girls? Are they all right?"

"One of them is in some rehabilitation program. The bodies of the other two girls were shipped back to their families."

"They were killed. *Dios mio.*"

"I don't know about the Serbian girl. She vanished."

"Good for her."

"One would hope. What are your plans?"

Reymond looked around the hospital room, as though it might provide an answer. He smoothed the sheets on his lap. "I have no idea, dude. Mom got me a lawyer. Don't know if he's any good but I don't know anyone better. What about you?"

"Janis made for a strong witness. She'll be an important ally for me. I think I'm going to be all right. I think."

Reymond snorted. "That's good news, but I meant do you know a good lawyer. Who's Janis?"

Trace shrugged. "A friend."

Reymond felt his head by running his fingers along the edge of the gauze, lightly pushing on it. "Bitch shot me point-blank. And yet here I am. Still breathing. Can you believe it?"

"Sure, why not."

Trace heard footsteps behind himself and turned around. It was Reymond's mother and sister. They brushed by Trace without acknowledging him. Reymond's mother carried a plate of food wrapped in tinfoil, the universal detail of any homecooked meal. Without a word, she set the plate on the stand next to his bed. She went to her surviving son and embraced him with one arm around his chest, the other around his neck. She kissed his bandaged head several times and whispered to him in Spanish. Reymond closed his eyes and savored his mother's touch. Her warmth. This son was still with her. There was still hope for him. Still a bigger reason for that journey she'd made so many years ago to give her family a new life.

"You a friend?" the sister asked Trace.

Trace nodded. "Of sorts," he said.

He turned to leave but Reymond called out to him. Trace turned back around to see his mother still holding on. Not letting go of this one. Not ever.

"You called the FBI?" Reymond asked him. "It was you, wasn't it?"

"I don't know what you're talking about. You need to get some rest."

"You called the FBI, didn't you? 'Fess up."

Trace cocked his finger at Reymond and winked. "Get well soon."

"I knew it! Getting shot in the head has given me

ESP! I can sense things now that I couldn't before. I'm psychic!"

On TV, a dinosaur was biting the head off one of the giant robots. Sparks fell from wires inside its neck as its head became separated. A crowd of people cheered this safely from a hillside.

Trace smirked. "What number am I thinking of?" he asked Reymond. "One to ten?"

"The number ten!"

I'll be damned.

—

After Trace left the room, he turned to visit the nursing station. He meant to ask them for Camila's new room number but nearly ran into a nurse walking by. He grabbed her arm, a bit rougher than he'd meant to. "The woman that was just in here," he said. He indicated her empty room. "You moved her again?"

The nurse looked into the room, then back at Trace. "Were you her husband?"

"No, I'm a friend. I'm here all the time."

"Camila?"

"Yes, her. Every time I come here, you guys have moved her somewhere else."

The nurse frowned as she faced him. "Camila passed away," she said. "She died last night. I'm so sorry."

Trace barked a quick laugh. "No, that's impossible. She was much better. She was almost out of here."

"I know who you're talking about."

"I don't think you do."

"Yes, Camila was improving, but she got a blood clot in her lungs, okay? This can often happen to patients with her type of injuries."

"So she's gone? No no no,…that's…"

The nurse shook her head. She waited to see if there was anything else required of her. When Trace failed to speak more, she turned and left. He reached out to stop her but missed. He let her walk away.

He went back to her hospital room and stood in the doorway. He took in the room and for a moment everything became remarkably vivid: the empty, white bed, his burned but healing hands, the window blinds making striped shadows across the floor, the dying flowers.

His phone buzzed and he took it out. It was Janis calling with another question for her article. He sent her to voicemail but decided he would call her back later. He had no one else to call, so why not. He was getting used to her.

Trace crawled onto Camila's bed and lay there alone, crumpled from feelings of overwhelming loneliness and abandonment. He mourned for Nora. He mourned for Camila. He mourned for the other slaves he'd seen shot. The thousands before and after them. He mourned for Enrique. He even mourned for Jason Shaw and his people. And their people. The world would swallow all of us. Existence was cold and uncomfortable. He curled up like a fetus in the light of the window and he cried, letting it go at last. He cried and he cried and wasn't sure when he'd ever stop. Maybe any second. Maybe never.

LEAVE A REVIEW

We would be extremely grateful if you could take just a minute to write a review on Amazon and/or Goodreads about this book. Even if the review is brief (2 or 3 sentences) that would be incredibly helpful. Recommending this book to a friend doesn't hurt either. :)

Thank you and we love you!!!

THE VAMPIRE IRREGULARS

Book One in The Tales of the Vampyr Series
Rory Penland

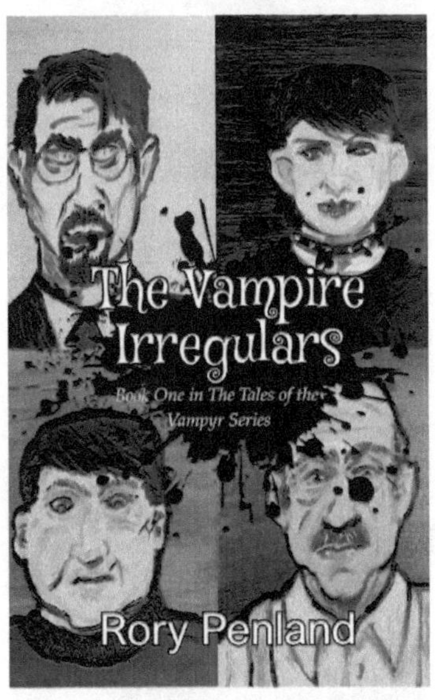

Prepare to have your perceptions of vampires shattered!

Gone are the days of timid creatures hiding in the shadows. Instead, behold The Vampire Irregulars—a breed of undead that defies conventions, craves the spotlight, and revels in the forbidden. This spellbinding anthology is a must-read for horror, fantasy, and vampire enthusiasts. Arm yourself with a crucifix and prepare for an electrifying ride that will leave you craving more.

Available now on Amazon, Barnes & Noble, and other major retailers!

DARK LORDS OF THE TRAILER PARK

Short Stories
Lee Anderson

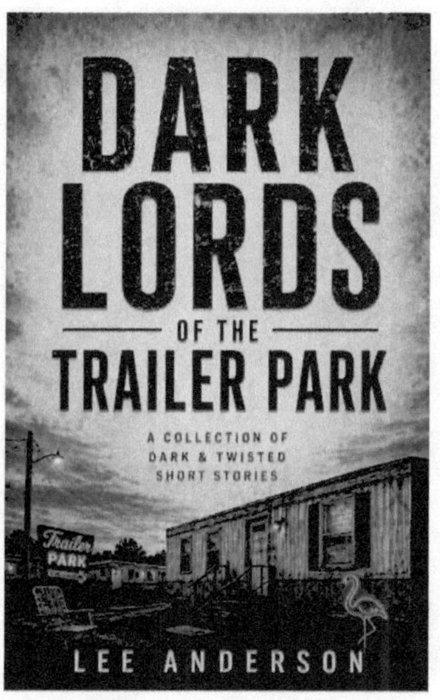

This gripping collection of stories will take you on a thrill ride through a morally bankrupt landscape of desire, desperation, and constant danger. *Dark Lords of the Trailer Park* is an exploration of redemption in unexpected places. A riveting deep dive into the complexities of human nature, the triumphs and challenges of society's outcasts. Lee Anderson's riveting tales will leave you breathless, yearning for more, long after the final page has turned.

Available now on Amazon, Barnes & Noble, and other major retailers!

WHAT HAPPENED AT SISTERS CREEK

A Horror Novel
Lee Anderson

A small-town sheriff sends a search party into the woods to hunt two escape convicts. What they find instead is a savage, unthinkable horror...

"I squirmed, I cringed, I gritted my teeth and held my breath...And that ending.... I just.... WHAT? I don't even know what to say. Amazing? Exhilarating? Total WTF moment? It was soooooo good!" Jessica Scurlock, author of **Pretty Lies**

"It was VISCERAL for me as a reader in a way that all great horror/thrillers are. You want to be in it and at the same time you want to run the hell away from it as fast as you can!" Amanda Nicole Ryan, author of **Keeper**

Available now on Amazon, Barnes & Noble,

and other major retailers!

BACHELOR'S GUIDE TO POST-APOCALYPTIC SUCCESS

Book One of the Post-Apocalyptic Bachelor Guides
Rory Penland

In a world destroyed by nuclear devastation, love becomes the ultimate test of survival.

Brandon Hoffner, a once-celebrated baseball prodigy, awakens from a frozen slumber to a horrifying reality. With only his loyal dog, Beau, at his side, he embarks on a dangerous journey across a desolate globe in search of fellow survivors. But his mission goes beyond companionship; he seeks a woman who can reignite humanity's fading spark.

Available now on Amazon, Barnes & Noble, and other major retailers!

Join our mailing list at

palmcirlepressbooks.com

to receive an unforgettable
FREE short story. Plus news and contests!

Hailing from Miami, Florida, Heather Wilde stepped into the dazzling world of fashion modeling at just 14, gracing runways and photo shoots for five unforgettable years. But the allure of storytelling soon eclipsed the runway lights, and Wilde's talent for words proved just as striking as her presence on stage.

An award-winning writer, Wilde claimed the prestigious Josephine Friedman Award for Short Fiction and took First Place in the Florida State Writers Association's National Fiction Contest. Her literary ambitions carried her to New York City, where she fearlessly reinvented herself. At the renowned agency Lippincott Mazzie McQuilkin, she flourished as a "writer-for-hire," captivating clients and readers alike with her narrative brilliance.

Now calling Manhattan's East Village home, Wilde channels her creative energy into her electrifying *South Beach Crime Thriller Series*. Whether spinning tales of intrigue or dreaming up her next big twist, she's always in good company—surrounded by a goldfish and two mischievous cats who can testify to Heather's brilliance.